MW00415481

PROTECTING HIS RUNAWAY

MEASHA STONE

STORMY NIGHT PUBLICATIONS

COPYRIGHT

Published by Stormy Night Publications and Design, LLC.
www.StormyNightPublications.com

Stone, Measha
Protecting His Runaway

1

Jacob St. Claire walked through the Museum of Science and Industry entrance as though he were King Tut himself. With his shoulders rolled back with confidence, his thick, graying hair slicked back away from his face, he strutted through the crowd until he finally found what he'd been hunting. His daughter.

Addison caught her father's eye through the thick crush of investors, charity mongrels, and politicians and froze. He'd been expecting her to meet him at his home so they could arrive at the fundraiser together. Appearances were extremely important to Jacob St. Claire, and having to search out his daughter didn't look good. Even from across the room, with dozens of people milling around between them, he could send a lightning strike of agitation through her.

"Addy, you okay?" Her lifelong friend, Charity, followed Addison's gaze. "Oh. He's pissed." She whispered the obvious.

Not many people would be able to look at Jacob and know exactly what he was thinking. Putting on a show for the public came first; his anger would have to wait. But Addison and Charity knew him, knew the little crinkle on the side of his mouth wasn't caused from a happy-to-be-here smile; no, anger boiled just below the surface.

Addison handed Charity her glass of wine and excused herself. Better to hurry to his side now than to make him continue stalking her. Going to him would alleviate some of his anger, but not all of it. Her father was an important man in the city. Sitting high on the committee of zoning, he could put businesses in business or out, depending on his mood, and their wallet size. Growing up she'd seen her father as a shining soldier, like most daughters did. He was her daddy after all, and daddies would always be heroes to their little girls. But as she'd grown up, she'd seen things, heard things, learned things that made the halo over her father's head less radiant, less straight until it was all but a rusted ring dangling from his shoulder.

"Hi, Daddy." She stepped up to him as he finished his conversation with another investor. He plastered on a large grin and leaned in to kiss her cheek.

"Addison." He gripped her shoulders, fingers

digging into her as he placed another kiss to her opposite cheek. "You were supposed to meet me at the house, you made me late." No one around them could hear him, and if they could, she wondered if his poisonous tone would give them the same skin-crawling sensation it did her.

It didn't matter. After tomorrow, she'd be free. Free of her father's attempts to control her life. Free of whatever arrangements he made for her future. No more wondering how he would react to a decision she'd made. He would be occupied, up to his receding hairline in legal trouble.

"I'm sorry. Charity picked me up, and we went for dinner before heading over." She curled her lips into the polite smile she'd perfected over the years. Her father didn't hold a senate seat or such power as that, but that didn't matter. There were plenty of people wanting to buy his votes, his cooperation, or his signature. He was well known in polite society, and other societies as well.

Just another day, and she'd be able to walk away.

"Jesse wanted to accompany us, but he needed to take care of something first. He'll be around a bit later." He checked his clunky Rolex and gave her a pinning look. "I assured him you'd be delighted to see him and to accompany him home."

"I wish you hadn't." Addison kept her voice low, hoping she was able to keep her disgust hidden. Just the name Jesse Stephanos made her skin crawl. Hearing that she was expected to accompany him anywhere set her hair to stand on end. "I'm going out with Charity in a bit. We have plans." Of course, he wouldn't approve, and she didn't expect him to; he never did.

"You need to accept your future."

She knew that tone, knew what it meant, and that arguing against it would be futile.

"Jesse's a good man."

Addison looked up at her father then. Good man? Did he even know what that meant anymore? Had he ever? "Daddy, I'm not ready." She tried to look away, but he gripped her arm. The tightness of his grip drew her attention back to him.

"It's been a year, Addison. I've let you grieve for that drug addict long enough. It's time for a new start. Jesse can give you that."

Addison stared down at where his hand held her, seeing the indents on her skin around his fat fingers. He must have realized where they were finally, and released her, rubbing her arm in almost an affectionate way. She wouldn't bruise, but she'd be sore the next day.

"I can't. I won't." She shook her head. On this subject, she wouldn't budge. She would not date Jesse Stephanos much less marry him, and after tomorrow, she wouldn't have to worry about that anymore. But the memory of Steven, her fiancé, her dead fiancé, would continue to hold onto her as the days passed. "He wasn't a drug user," she mumbled, knowing her father's anger would only increase with her insistence.

Steven had never so much as smoked a cigarette. No way had Steven driven himself into that wall on I90, too high to even see it coming. It hadn't happened that way, no matter what the police report or her father had said. Steven's sin hadn't been drugs; it had been trying to marry her. If his brakes hadn't been used, it's because they hadn't been working.

"Mr. St. Claire!" A stout man with graying hair interrupted them, holding his hands out in greeting. Addison stepped aside to allow the man full access to her father. She stood idly by while the two exchanged pleasantries. "I was hoping I'd run into you tonight." At that, Addison looked to her father, having been trained much like Pavlov's dogs to salivate at the idea of escape whenever those words were uttered in her presence.

"Well, then I'm glad I made the trip this evening. Addison, my dear, why don't you find Charity. I'm sure she's waiting for you."

"Yes, Daddy."

He added, "Don't go too far though." She gave a quick nod and shuffled off into the crowd seeking out the safety of a corner.

Addison found a secluded spot near a dessert table

and snatched a glass of wine from a waiter walking by; it wasn't strong enough, but it would do.

"Hey, there you are." Charity slid up to her side. "I was beginning to think I was going to have to actually go over by your father." She gave a weak smile and pushed back a thick curl from her face. Charity stayed as clear of her father as Addison wished she could.

"Someone wanted to do business, I was sent away." Addison drained the last bit of Pinot from the glass.

"Are we staying, leaving, or are you attached to him now that he found you?" Charity hated the social scene, especially when Addison's father arrived. Her own father sat on a city board, but didn't do much work with Addison's father. The pressure to be the perfect daughter never applied to Charity. Her parents already believed she was the perfect daughter. Unlike Addison, who was under constant attack and surveillance.

She took a deep breath and reminded herself it was only for another night. One more night. Come tomorrow afternoon, she'd be clear of the lies, the corruption, all of it. She'd be able to go out without her father's men tailing her, tattling her every move to him. She could go to a club, could play with a man and not worry he'd end up with a broken nose the next day. She wouldn't have to hear about how sick and perverted her life was, and how ashamed he was of her, or listen to any more threats of having her committed to a hospital that would clean her of all of her whorish ways. Her father never understood, and there was no point in trying to explain anymore.

She was twenty-four years old. She didn't need to explain to him, she just needed to get the hell away from him.

One more night, then she'd have her meeting. Her stomach twisted at the idea. Going to the police station would take every bit of courage she had in her. Going against her father, against the Stephanos family, wasn't something she'd considered lightly.

"Addison." Charity touched her shoulder. "What's up? Why are you so tense tonight?"

Addison threw on a smile, knowing Charity would see right through it. "Nothing. I'm okay. Just tired." Emotionally and physically, but she wouldn't go into details. The less Charity actually knew, the better.

"Guess who?" Jackson, Charity's boyfriend, popped up behind Charity and covered her eyes. It was a childish game, one they'd played since high school when they met.

As usual, Charity giggled and guessed incorrectly, rattling off the names of which ever celebrity she fancied at that moment. Jackson gave her a playful swat to her backside, careful no one but the three of them saw, and spun her around to kiss her.

Addison watched the two of them with the same envy as she'd had when they started dating in school.

Even after four years of college spent mostly on opposite sides of the state, they managed to keep their relationship steady. During all the stress and deadlines,
Jackson had been Charity's rock. And when Addison
had lost the only thing that mattered to her, had lost
Steven, he'd been her rock, too.

"Hey, Jackson." Addison hugged him. "Wasn't
expecting you."

"Yeah. I told Charity I probably wouldn't make it,
but I needed a break." In his last year of law school,
Jackson spent most of his time with his nose buried in
books.

"I can't wait for you to finish." Charity ran her
hand over his cheek, pushing away his dark hair.

"A few more months." He smiled down at her,
curling an arm around her waist and pulling her close
to him. "I can only stay an hour. What have you girls
got planned tonight?"

Addison glanced back over at her father. Had he
taken the hint that she wasn't going anywhere with
Jesse Stephanos, or would he still be expecting her to
obey him, like some little girl? She caught sight of
Jesse walking into the room, his thick black hair
slicked back from his olive-skinned face, his dark
tailored suit making him look even darker, and he
headed straight for her father.

Her stomach clenched when he reached him.

Jacob shooed away the man he was talking with and gave his full attention to the little sleaze of a man.

The two were in a heated discussion. Whatever Jesse was telling him didn't make her father happy. Charity was talking, but Addison's attention was focused solely on her father.

Another man, one older, thinner than her father walked up to the pair and joined their discussion. Jesse made introductions, hands were shaken, and the conversation continued. More heated stares between Jesse and her father, and then her father started to look around the crowded room. For her, he was looking for her.

"What's your father doing talking to Detective Jamison?" Jackson asked with more than a little curiosity. Addison's heart dropped into her stomach, her breath caught in her throat.

"Probably just getting a bribe." Charity laughed, but kept her voice low. The three of them knew what sort of person Addison's father was, and in any other circumstance Addison probably would have just rolled her eyes. But that name meant something. Something horrible for her.

"That's Detective Jamison?" She gripped the wineglass even harder as she watched her father still scanning the room for her.

"Addy? You okay?" Charity asked, no more levity in her voice.

"I have to go." She plunked her glass down on the table beside her and ran for the nearest exit. She heard Charity calling after her, heard Jackson's voice follow her, but she didn't stop. She couldn't. Not now. She had to go, to run. Get out of the city and right this moment. Not tomorrow. Not the next day. Right now.

Because her future, the one she'd been counting on—the one she kept telling herself was only a day away—was standing in that damn museum with her father, telling him, and that creep Jesse, everything she'd already implied, and all about their meeting scheduled for the next day.

Just before she ran through the doorway toward a back exit, she looked over her shoulder. Her father's brown eyes caught hers. Hatred. Anger. Betrayal lurked there. Her heart stopped, but her feet didn't. Without another glance, she ran from the room, from the museum, and from her life.

2

Sporting a headache and an angry stomach, Trevor Stringer walked into his office carrying a mug of freshly brewed coffee, black. Maybe a few sips would straighten out his body chemistry, strip away whatever alcohol lingered from the night before.

Just as he sat down at his desk and flipped on his computer, his commanding officer walked in, shutting the door behind him. That was not a good sign. Either he'd pissed off someone and didn't remember doing it, or he was about to be given a shitty assignment.

Not that any assignment in missing persons was a vacation. Chasing after lost kids who more often than not ended up in a body bag than back home with their family had left him jaded. If Cowsky was closing his office door, the case was a shit show.

"Long night?" Cowsky asked with a hint of humor in his voice.

Taking a slow sip of the near burnt coffee, Trevor nodded. "Yeah. Those bachelor parties really get out of hand quick." He quietly put his cup down on his desk and ran his hand over his chin. He hadn't shaved. Hell, he had barely managed to button his damn shirt.

"No one said you needed to help close down the bar with those kids." Cowsky had attended the party along with half the department to celebrate Winston's last hurrah before settling down with his high-school sweetheart. But Cowsky had had the good sense to leave at a reasonable hour and get more than three hours' sleep, and he hadn't helped finish off the bottle of Jack Daniel's either.

"You're not in here to comment on my partying skills." Trevor picked up his coffee again, taking a whiff and deciding against trying to stomach the brew. "What's going on?"

His commander sighed. "Jacob St. Claire, you know him?"

"Heard of him." Trevor leaned back in his chair, thankful that the lights weren't on in the room, and only a bare trace of sunlight was peeking in through the blinds. "One of the zoning guys, or something. A friend of a friend had dealings with the zoning committee when trying to open a new club."

"He's the chair of that committee." Cowsky nodded. "His daughter's missing."

Shitty assignment it is, Trevor decided. Chairman on any committee in the city would be a high-profile case. "How long? How old is she?" Trevor pulled his yellow pad in front of him and snagged a pen from the cup on his desk.

"She's twenty-four. Been missing two months." Cowsky walked around the desk to the window, and using his fingers to pry open the blinds, he looked out into the parking lot.

Trevor's hand stilled over the paper. "Two months? Did he wait that long to report it or are you handing me a cold trail?" The case could be coming out of another house, and if they had fucked it up, he would be the next in line to clean up their fucking mess. He wasn't in the mood for other people's sloppiness.

"No." Cowsky let go of the blinds, the plastic snapping back into place. His thick-rimmed glasses hid his eyes well enough that Trevor couldn't really make out what he was thinking, but the way he stuffed his hands into his pockets and ran his tongue over his lower teeth said enough.

"No, what? No, he didn't wait two months, no, there isn't a cold trail? What?" Trevor had been on the force for nearly ten years, joined up the day after he turned eighteen. Two weeks after his mother died from gunshot wounds, which she received while working as a nurse in a hospital. And in those ten years he'd seen some crazy shit, horrible shit, things he didn't think humans were capable of doing to each other. And a parent's betrayal wasn't one of the worst things. "What is it? Out with it." He rubbed his temples. The stress of the conversation made his head throb harder.

"He knows where she is." And there it was.

"How can she be missing if he knows where she is?"

Cowsky shook his head. "She's hiding out in Eagle, Michigan, working at a club out there. She's cut off all communication with him; he's worried. He wants her to come home."

"Why not just go get her then?" Trevor asked, already knowing he didn't want to know the reason.

"It's complicated."

"Complicated? She's twenty-four, you said? She's out there working? She's not missing, and she's an adult. Why are we getting involved?"

"He doesn't want press." He shrugged.

"Then filing a missing person's report probably wasn't the way to go." His gut twisted. Something was wrong. This wasn't just a politician asking for a favor, there was a reason this girl wouldn't come home.

"It's unofficial. No file is being started, no report has been placed. He wants someone to go get her and bring her home. Someone who she doesn't know, who won't startle her into running off again."

"Wait a minute." Trevor stood up from his chair and confronted his boss. "Are you telling me that you want me to go fetch her and bring her home, in an unofficial capacity? What if she doesn't want to come home? Surely, he has goons of his own. I've seen some shit in the papers about his suspected dealings." Now that his mind was clearing, the name Jacob St. Claire rang more bells.

"Look. I don't know. I'm doing what I'm told because the higher ups say to. I don't really give a shit either. I just want this done and over, this shit makes my stomach turn. You know that."

Trevor nodded. Cowsky was as strait-laced as they came. If he was bringing this bullshit to him, it wasn't because he wanted to get involved. "So why me? If it's a catch and release, send Thompson or that new guy —Jimbo or whatever."

Cowsky laughed. "Jim Bob, and no. The club she's working at, it's not their scene."

Now that got his attention.

"What do you mean by that?" he asked. Cowsky and he did not hang out with the same crowds after shift, but they'd known each other long enough for Cowsky to know a few personal details that the rest of their department didn't, or at least had the good sense not to mention.

"She's working at one of those S&M clubs—a professional bottom or some shit. St. Claire didn't go into much more detail than that. Poor bastard, I thought he was gonna lose his lunch just saying the few things he did."

Trevor had heard of the profession, but never looked into it. He didn't need to. Paying someone to play wasn't necessary for him any more than needing to pick up some street walker on the corner.

"They could always pick her up at her apartment, or hotel, or wherever the fuck she's staying." Just because he was familiar with the BDSM world didn't make him the best cop for the job.

Cowsky's reluctant smile pushed into a frown. The facade of this being an easygoing conversation broke.

"Look, that girl won't come home on her own. I don't know details, but I've heard enough about St. Claire to suspect why she ran off in the first place. You know as well as I do there are cops around here that answer to the green badge much more than the gold one hanging off their belt. I want this girl brought home safe."

"If you think St. Claire's a danger to her, why ask me to bring her back here at all?" Trevor asked. His patience thinned with each new detail.

"The boss says to do this for St. Claire. You go. You make sure she's safe and sound, then bring her back. One day tops. If she gives you reason to believe it's a danger coming back to Daddy, well, like you said. She's an adult, and this is an unofficial job," Cowsky said, shrugging his shoulders.

"And if my ass gets twisted up in some shit storm over all this?" Trevor asked, knowing it was a very strong possibility, because if that girl had good cause to stay away from Daddy, a shit storm would be right around the corner.

"Like you said, it's a catch and release. Get up there, grab the girl, and bring her home. Then it's over. You going, I know it's a done deal. These other fucks... hell." He combed a hand through his hair and looked straight at him. "She's pretty, intelligent, and a spoiled brat from what I'm told. She probably took off after a family fight or something stupid. These other guys, they won't know how to handle her. And since it's not official, and she's not underage..."

"Oh, I see. Technically, you're asking me to kidnap her and bring her back to Daddy. And since she doesn't want to be around Daddy, she's not going to come easily." It was all forming in his mind better now, and he suddenly wished he could crawl back inside the Jack Daniel's bottle. He hated brats and spoiled ones were the worst kind. "So, why'd she run? Daddy wouldn't pay her credit card bill or something?"

"I have no idea." Cowsky spread his hands out to indicate he was telling the truth. "Like I said, she's an adult. If it turns out that she's not just some runaway brat, use your best judgement."

Trevor tried to gauge his boss's expression to decide which way he suspected it was going to go down. "You're going back and forth here. Either she took off because she's scared of her father and you're sending me on some harebrained rescue mission, or she's a spoiled brat who needs to be dragged back to Daddy. Which is it?"

"You know, you're being a much bigger pain in the ass than I thought you'd be about this." Cowsky's eyebrows furrowed. "The girl may need help. If I send someone else and that is the case, I don't know that the right thing will be done. With you, I have no doubts."

"And if I do drag her back here and she cries kidnapping? This is all unofficial, what saves my ass from rotting in jail? Not to mention the little detail that she has every right to stay away from her father no matter what the reason," Trevor pointed out.

Cowsky regarded him in heavy silence for a long moment.

"I'll save your ass. If this goes badly, you have my backing. You have my word," Cowsky said.

It was Trevor's turn to inspect him. Cowsky's jaw tightened, though the loose skin around his chin trembled a hair. Obviously, this crap left an unsavory taste in his mouth as much as it did Trevor. The stubble on his face seemed grayer than usual; the extra weight around his middle seemed to drag him down a little more, too.

"Just please, get it done. I'll forward you the details I received. Take the day to rest up, then head out. Let's get this done by Monday." Without waiting for Trevor to agree, he left, softly closing the door behind him.

Regardless of how much the situation pissed him off, Trevor wouldn't put any more argument into it. Cowsky was one of the few Trevor still trusted.

He hated brats, but he'd pick this one up, he'd bring her home to Daddy, and he'd move on to the next case. Maybe one with an actual purpose.

HER FATHER WOULDN'T GIVE up. Addison pulled her long blonde hair back to the nape of her and began braiding it. After getting out of Chicago and finally settling in a small no-name town, she'd considered dying her hair and chopping it off. But she wouldn't let her father take anything else away from her. She'd already lost enough because of him, and he never saw how much it all hurt her. Not after he'd threatened to call in a few favors with his friends on the board of education if she didn't stick to teaching in Chicago, not after he'd frozen her trust fund in order to keep her complacent, not even after Steven was murdered. He'd left her life in shambles, and all with one myopic purpose. To keep her in Chicago.

She'd been a fool to believe he'd just let her leave town and start over somewhere else. The idea of her leaving Chicago was what had turned him so violently against Steven in the first place.

And there was the Stephanos family. It was bad enough her father had dealings with that scum, but to start actually pushing for her to marry one of them? Even for him, it seemed off.

She wouldn't, couldn't do that. No matter her situation, she would not give herself over to a family even more corrupt than her father. Men like Jesse and his father, Carmine, weren't a special breed. They were the only type of men her father did business with. She'd seen them enough growing up to know what sort they were. Dangerous. But the day Steven was ripped from her, the moment she'd lost her fiancé to the greed of men like her father and the Stephanos family, was the day she would no longer play their game.

"There's a guy outside asking about you." Claire poked her head into Addison's tiny office. If it could really be called that. The water closet turned manager office didn't exactly feel like home.

"He asked for me by name?" Addison threw her braid back over her shoulder once the rubber band was in place. She hadn't used her real name. She had grown up with Jacob St. Claire as her father; she knew better.

"No. Well, not really." Claire tucked a strand of her bleached blonde hair behind her ear and slid the pocket door of the room all the way open to make way for her to step in. In a hushed voice, she continued. "He asked for Addison St. Claire, but he described you to a T."

"Just tell him there's no Addison here." Addison pulled the braid in front of her again and removed the rubber band, pulling her fingers through the plaited hair and unleashing it once again.

"He has a picture of you," Claire whispered.

In the two months Addison had been away from her father, she'd managed to make somewhat of a life for herself in the dinky-ass town. Going by the name of Maria Sanchez, which really didn't fit her at all, she'd gotten a job as night supervisor at the Boom Boom Club, a fully nude strip club two miles off the main highway that catered to the kinkier lifestyles. It hadn't even been hard. Mr. Garren, the owner of the club, hadn't bothered to look at her application or check any of her references. She knew the lifestyle, and she didn't ask questions about the back-room business, other than where he wanted the cash deposited. He'd hired her on the spot.

Claire was not only one of the strippers, but she also worked in the back rooms as a professional bottom. She took a solid spanking or flogging at least once a night.

The temptation had been there for Addison. A solid ass warming might have done her a world of good, but she wasn't going to bend over for just any man, no matter how good the pay was.

"Claire, my name isn't Addison. It's Maria." She leaned over her desk and raised her eyebrows. "Maria Sanchez. I don't know who Addison is."

"I could have sworn your father had some long-lost ancestor in Normandy. Sanchez sounds a bit more Hispanic, and your pale complexion suggests something a little further north," a deep voice said from behind Claire.

Claire, to her credit, didn't squeal in her moment of panic. Her eyes widened, and she slowly looked over her shoulder, but she didn't say anything.

"I'm sorry, but you can't be back here." Addison stood from her desk and rounded it, making sure not to kick the leg as she did almost every other time she shimmied around the damn thing. She motioned for Claire to go, and she quickly scurried along, leaving Addison to deal with whatever asshole her father had probably sent. How her father even figured out where she was didn't matter. She wasn't going home. Not today, not ever.

"I'll be where I need to be." Arrogance filled his tone.

He stepped closer to the door, the light fixture directly over his head illuminating his face. A set jaw, chiseled features, and the darkest eyes she'd ever seen on a man were all directed at her. Addison wasn't a short girl, and yet he still seemed to tower over her.

His hand moved up between them, showing her a picture he held in his hand. It was her, taken a month before she'd packed up what she needed and got out of Chicago. "You don't hide all that well, Addison. Cutting your hair, dying it, shit, putting on a pair of fake glasses would have at least shown some effort."

He was mocking her.

She snatched the photo from his hand, delighting in the surprise that flashed in his eyes, and tore the picture in half, then in half again. "No Addison here. Sorry to have wasted your time. Jimmy here will show you out." She waved a hand and the bouncer, who Claire finally had the good sense to go get, walked down the hall toward them.

"Uh, Jimmy, was it?" He didn't seem worried in the least. He turned to Jimmy and pulled something out of his back pocket. Opening up what looked like a wallet, he flashed it in the air, making Jimmy halt in his step. When she tried to take it from his hand like she had the picture, he caught her wrist in a tight grip.

"Jimmy, can you get him out of here?" Addison tried to wrench her wrist free, but his fingers were digging too hard into her for her to achieve anything other than hurting herself more.

"Jimmy! Get up here!" The radio on Jimmy's hip hissed to life. "Now!" The panicked call for help concerned her, and she tried to step forward, to get out of the back and see what was going on in the club. The stranger wouldn't have it; he clamped his hand around her arm and pulled her back, shoving her behind him.

A shot rang out, screaming started, and Addison shoved his back. "I have to see what's going on!" She clawed at him when he pushed her against the wall with his back and retrieved a pistol from his side. "What are you doing?"

He looked at her over his shoulder, a dark, eerie gaze. "You stay here. Don't move a muscle, princess." He strode to where the heavy black curtains closed off the front of the club from the back offices, and with one finger pushed aside the curtain enough to peer out. She heard more screaming, another shot. Not one to stand idly by, she ran to the curtain and pulled it out of his hands to see.

Two large men—not in the muscular way like Mr. Stranger Danger, but fat instead—moved through the club. She could see Jimmy lying on the floor at the front, blood pouring from his chest. They were looking around. When the taller of the two caught her gaze, recognition hit her hard and she stumbled back.

"I said to stay put." Stranger Danger yanked her back, the curtain falling back into place.

"Stephanos... cousins. Fuck."

He didn't bother to wait for an explanation; he grabbed her hand and yanked her to follow him toward the back entrance.

"Wait. I need to get my stuff."

No answer from him except to pull harder on her arm. He kicked open the back door and pulled her through, shoving her into the back lot just as another shot rang out. Louder, and much closer. Debris from the concrete wall that was hit flew out the door, landing on her shoulders. When she looked back, all she saw were the angry fiery eyes of her stranger.

"Move. There." He pointed to a car, a sedan, parked beside her own car.

"I don't have my keys," she muttered as she followed him.

"Not that car, mine." He opened the passenger door of his car and glared at her. She didn't move. Leaving with him could be dangerous. She didn't know who he was, or who had sent him. If her father had sent him, then why the Stephanos cousins, too?

"Get in, princess. We don't have time for you to have a fit. Get in the fucking car." His voice was low, and his lips were pressed together so tightly she wondered if they'd bruise. When she still didn't move, he grabbed her arm and maneuvered her until she was in the front seat. "You move and you'll regret it," he said firmly, but not with a raised voice.

The back door of the club opened just as he ran around to his own side of the car. She watched the Stephanos cousins huffing as they tried to hurry to the car, but her stranger had already turned it on and was reversing. She screeched when he almost hit one of the cousins, and then changed gears before tearing out of the lot.

Once they were clear of the lot and driving up the ramp of the highway, she turned back around in the seat and took a few gulping breaths.

"Seatbelt," he said.

She turned to look at him. She'd just been pulled out of her work by some strange man, two killers had almost snatched her, and he was worried about her seatbelt?

"Now, princess." His hardened tone combined with the heated look he shot at her got her moving. She knew nothing about him, except he had saved her from those Stephanos goons. For that reason, and only that reason, did she snap the belt over her chest.

"My name is Maria," she huffed. "And my apartment is off the next exit." She pointed to the sign signaling the upcoming ramp. The darkness of the evening filtered out most of the street lighting, but she could still make out the exit.

He laughed. "You aren't going back to your apartment, sweetheart. Those guys are probably on their way there. If they found you at the club, they'll find your address quick enough."

"Then get me there before them so I can get my things." She pointed again to the ramp.

"I said no." He stated the fact as though that should end the conversation. Well, he obviously didn't know who he'd just abducted.

"I don't know who you are, or what the fuck you want with me, but I'm done playing this fucking game." She unhooked her belt and lurched to his side of the car, yanking the wheel and trying to steer them toward the ramp.

He pried her hands off the wheel, shoved her back to her side of the car, and straightened out the car without missing a beat. With a ragged breath, she kicked the glovebox.

"Pull over!" she demanded, kicking it again.

"Settle down," he barked at her. "I'm not pulling over, I'm not taking you back to your apartment, and I'm not letting you destroy my fucking car."

"Let me out! You asshole! Who are you anyway! Why are you here?"

"Your dad sent me, princess. Time to stop having a hissy fit and go back home to Daddy."

If he thought that statement would gain her cooperation, he lacked a few facts.

3

Trevor was no stranger to the spoiled brat of the upper class in Chicago. In the years he had worked in missing persons, he'd been sent on more than one wild goose chase to hunt down the kid who ran away because they weren't satisfied with their privileges, or because they were seeking the attention of their parents who were too busy playing the socialite or banging the investors' daughters to see to their own kids.

One kid, Jason, had flown the coop over his birthday present. Turning sixteen should have meant a shiny new BMW or Mercedes, but when he was given only a mere Lexus, he took his temper tantrum to the north side of the city and holed up in a hotel room. He wasn't hard to find, once reported missing.

Trevor had checked his credit card purchases—something his brilliant parents hadn't thought to do. He'd knocked on his door within an hour and Jason, looking smug, went home willingly, after his parents had promised him a better car.

And while Trevor had wasted a day and a half on Jason's little tantrum, a real missing kid was being tortured in the basement of a complete lunatic. The rookie who had been put on that case hadn't gotten to him in time. His body had washed up on the North Avenue beach the afternoon Jason had taken his friends on a joy ride in his brand-new BMW convertible.

The surprised gasp that came out of Addison's mouth didn't fit the smugness he'd become accustomed to with these people.

"I'm an adult. You can't just take me back, you don't have the right. I'm not a little girl!" From the corner of his eye he saw the pout of her lips and wanted to laugh. He would have, if the anger wasn't so hot in her eyes. She wasn't wrong either. She was well over the legal age. She could run way if she wanted to; hell, it technically wasn't running away. As an adult, she'd moved.

"Look. Your dad is worried. I was asked to come get you."

"You don't understand." She tugged on his arm.

He shot her a warning glare. "I do understand. Perfectly. Maybe Daddy didn't put enough in your trust fund, maybe he didn't buy you a big enough condo for your birthday. Whatever the problem is, I understand that instead of working a real case, helping a real person in trouble, I'm off dragging home some fucking princess!"

She pulled back at his words, probably because he'd lowered his voice into a stern, dominant tone for most of it. He hadn't meant to dip into dominant mode, that wasn't usually the way he did things. Not with his cases, and sure as hell not with a woman he didn't even know.

"W-what do you mean, working a real case?" Her question came out soft, curious more than angry.

He pulled out the same wallet he had flashed at the bouncer at the club and flipped it open, displaying his badge. "I'm a detective. Chicago PD."

She didn't react to his statement for a full minute. He felt her staring at him, and when he turned away from the road to glance at her, she didn't even look away.

"I can't go back to Chicago. Obviously, I can't stay where I was either." She bent over, resting her head on the glove compartment door, taking deep breaths. "He's really going to do it. I mean, I figured he would, that's why I took it—to protect myself."

"What are you talking about?" He changed lanes on the nearly empty highway.

"I can't go back to Chicago. Please, can't you just drop me off at a train station or something? I just, I can't. Not because of any reason you think. But I can't." When she looked up at him, her eyes were wide with something he rarely saw in one of his runaways. Terror. Most were annoyed, tired, or pissed that they'd been found, but he'd never encountered such fear in their eyes at the prospect of going home.

"Give me the reason. Tell me why, and I'll consider it."

"You can't take me back. I'm an adult," she said.

"You're starting to sound like a broken record. I'm driving, the car's pointed to Chicago, so yeah, I can take you back, adult or not." That part was true. He could, and would, if she wouldn't start cooperating. At the very least, he'd call the station and get this little family squabble off his hands.

"Why do you think my father sent you? Because those guys that shot up the fucking club, they work with him. Not directly for him, but they work for his associates, and they want me home, too. So, if he sent you, he is either trying to get to me before they do, or he wants me back so he can hand me over."

"None of that makes sense." With his pinky finger, he turned on his signal, making his way toward the exit.

"You don't understand." She looked out the back of the car. "Please, just turn around and get me back to my apartment. I have to get something. Something important."

"Well, if it's important, then your friends there will have it before you get back there."

"They can't find it. I need to get it before they do." She shook her head.

"What is it?"

She let out a loud sigh. "Just pull over and let me go." She tried once more, but he was already driving down the ramp that led them off the highway.

He would regret it, he knew it, but he couldn't seem to convince himself to do otherwise. Something in her voice, the slight tremble when she talked about her father, and the fear so prominent in her eyes when she looked at him, desperation underlying her pleas for him to let her go, reminded him that he was supposed to be one of the good guys. He'd been picked for this shit assignment for just that reason.

She hadn't run away because she didn't like her birthday gift. That much he got, that much he could bank on.

"You'll find I'm much easier to deal with when you behave. And right now, that means telling me the truth about what you're stashing at your apartment. Drugs?" He didn't really suspect that, she looked too clean-cut, too healthy to be mixed up with that shit.

"No. Information. I have information that I need to keep with me. If they get it and they get me, I'm as good as dead." She looked out the window as he drove down the off-ramp and took them onto darkened back roads.

Silence stretched out between them.

"Can you get me there from here without the highway?" He couldn't believe he was even entertaining the idea, let alone going along with it, but there was definitely something more to this whole situation than her dad had led him to believe. St. Claire and the Stephanos family working together in this little venture of retrieving an errant daughter? Didn't add up to him.

"Yes, absolutely." Hope sprang into her voice, and she sat up straighter in her seat. He sighed; most likely he was driving them right into a fucking trap. But if what she had hidden contained anything worth the Stephanoses chasing her down for, he wanted to get his eyes on it first.

He followed her directions down long deserted roads, and then through an area of town that looked more like a Stephen King novel than a real town. "You live here?" he asked, ducking his head to get a better look out the windshield.

Houses no bigger than a garage lined the street, damn near crumbling from the slight breeze.

"It's not fancy, but it keeps me out of the rain." She

didn't look at him, just pointed for him to make a right turn down a barely lit street.

He slowed the car to look for other traffic. They appeared to be the only ones awake on the street, but appearances were never solid enough leads.

"That place?" He pulled to the curb of an apartment building. Rather a house that had been turned into an apartment building. It looked barely large enough for a family to live in the entire building let alone to be split in four the way it was.

"I'll be right back." She reached for the handle, but Trevor pulled her back.

"No. You'll stay here. I'll go, you just tell me what I'm looking for."

She yanked her arm out of his grasp and sighed. "No. You'll take forever to find it. I'll just run in and run back out."

He scoffed. "Right, or you'll just run out the back yard and I'll have to chase you down and get all sweaty. I already had my run for the day, not in the mood to go for another. I'll go with you."

"Where the fuck am I going to go? I have no car and you saw what a desolate place this is." She jerked a thumb toward the window. She had a point there. Outside the last few blocks of houses, they were completely surrounded by farm land and deserted plots.

Trevor wasn't in the habit of explaining himself. He'd said he'd go with her and that's what was going to happen. She would either accept it and go along, or she wouldn't. That decision was on her.

Resting his hand on his handgun he placed himself in front of her door while he took a broad look around. No other cars, no lights on in any of the apartments, by all accounts they were alone. He reached back and opened the door, signaling for her to get out and be quiet.

"Stay behind me," he ordered and un-holstered his weapon. He didn't miss the eye roll, but it wasn't the time to correct her. There'd be plenty of time for that later, while she was explaining every bit of why she ran away from home.

She pointed out her door, the top floor. Of course. It couldn't be easy and be on the first floor. He nodded and headed up the rickety steps, hoping they'd hold both of them as they climbed. Beside the paint chipped in a hundred or so spots, the steps were warped and he noticed the wood rotting in too many places.

Why the hell she stayed in a place like that when she had money coming out of her ass didn't make a lick of sense. But it would. By the end of the fucking night she would tell him everything.

ADDISON PULLED her key out of her pocket and tried to shimmy past Trevor, but he only gave her a hard glare and took the key from her hand. The man was entirely too cautious.

Even if the Stephanos cousins knew where she lived, they couldn't have gotten from the club and back to her place before she and Stranger Danger did. He was overreacting.

Still. It didn't hurt to let him go into the darkened apartment first. He did have a gun after all.

The door stuck when he pushed. The cool fall temperature didn't seem to matter, the damn door swelled constantly. She watched him thrust his hip into the door and rolled her eyes.

"Let me—" Her shove against his body did nothing to move him, but gave her plenty of information as to how well built he was. The leanness of his body hid the fact that he was all muscle beneath his clothes.

He raised a dark eyebrow at her when she looked up at him, baffled as to how he hadn't even flinched when she'd shoved at him.

"This is your last warning, Addison. Behave, do what you're told, or you will regret it."

Now that threw her off balance. Who the hell did he think he was, threatening her like that? "You don't get to make those kind of threats."

"What threat? It's a god damn promise. Now stand over there, and let me get this door open."

"And if there's a trick to it? You won't let me tell you because you're some big man, some hard ass that can't take a simple direction from a woman, is that it?" She threw her hands in the air when his expression darkened even more. No sense pushing her luck.

"What's the trick?" he asked once she'd stepped to the other side of the small landing. A hint of annoyance lurked in his stare, but she chose to ignore it. The man really needed to lighten up. The situation was stressful enough without his attitude.

"You have to hit the door right above the handle, then shove from the center. It would be faster to just let me do it." She squirmed her way back into the doorway, and he let her push his hand out of the way. She doubted she would have succeeded without his cooperation. Using the side of her fist, she hit the door three inches above the door handle, then threw her shoulder into the door as she turned the knob. The door popped free of the frame and she flashed him a triumphant smile before stepping into the apartment.

She managed to get four steps in before his large hand clamped around her arm and yanked her back to him. His chest crashed into her back, nearly knocking the wind out of her.

"Wait here." He gave her arm a squeeze then walked past her, taking a look around the apartment.

"You might see better if you had a light on," she called out to him when she heard his foot bang into what she assumed was her dresser. Thankfully, she had been doing laundry that afternoon, so she knew none of her dirty clothes were lying around the room. Not that she really cared if he saw the room in the usual shambles she kept it in.

Steps on the stairs outside caught her attention, and she pushed herself against the wall, leaving the door open. Closing it would only signal her presence.

She picked up the glass vase she'd bought at a clearance sale the day before from the counter and held it to her chest. One step, two steps, each one closer than the next.

"Bitch better be here. I'm tired of chasing her scrawny ass."

She recognized that voice well enough to know that she needed the element of surprise more than ever. If he saw her, he'd get a shot in before she could scream.

Raising the vase over her head, she waited, hoping no one could hear the hammering of her heart. A long shadow cast over the entrance of the apartment, and the silhouette of one of the Stephanos cousins loomed in the doorway. Biting her lip hard, she tried to wait for him to step in, a little closer so she could reach his head from behind.

The creaking of a door opening in her room caught his attention and he stepped forward, heading toward the sound. Not waiting another second, she brought the vase down, hard. She never expected to hear such a raw sound like the breaking of bone as she did when the vase caught his skull at the perfect angle. Blood splattered over her arms and the floor around him as he fell face first onto the floor.

Panicked, she tossed the vase to the floor and cut to the door. She heard her name being yelled, but she wasn't stopping. She needed to get the fuck out of there. Luckily no one was on the stairs, no car idled nearby with more of Stephanos cousins, but there was no way for her drive out of there either. Deciding fleeing on foot was better than nothing, she cut through the gangway and headed toward the main road.

Nothing but open land stretched in front of her, and other than her own breathing she couldn't hear a sound. So, when her shirt was pulled backward, yanking her entire body back, she screamed and began to flail her arms. Throwing her fists and trying to kick her legs while scrambling out of the grip of whatever monster held her, she demanded to be let go.

"Leave me alone!" She tried to turn, to get her nails into her assailant, but the strong arm that crossed over her chest, immobilizing her against him, stopped her from any level of success.

"Stop it now, Addison." The dark voice, the firm order, could only have come from Trevor.

In her haste to get out of the apartment after

seeing and hearing what she'd done, she had forgotten about him. Her body went limp, but only for a moment before she tried to wiggle free again. His hold was too tight, and she was too close to him, could smell too much of him and feel too much body.

"Stop," he said again, giving her a little shake. "Just take a second and breathe." He didn't loosen his hold, but he softened his voice for her.

"Is he dead?" she asked between harsh breaths.

"I don't know." His fingers stroked her arms. "Just breathe." He let her go long enough to grasp her shoulders and turn her to face him. She expected to see anger, irritation at least, but instead she found a wrinkled brow and focused eyes. "Better?"

"I killed him." The words escaped her in a heated breath, but still didn't register fully. She'd taken a life. His blood stained her clothes; she could feel the sticky mess of it on her arms.

"We'll worry about that later. Come on, let's get back to the car." He kept her trapped up against him as he walked them back through the open field to her apartment building. "Your neighbors must sleep like the dead," he commented as they walked past the darkened windows.

"No one lives in the other apartments," she said. "Did you find my folder?" Pulling out of his hold, she turned toward him. Without that folder, she had nothing, no protection from her father, nothing to shield her from being blackmailed into marriage with one of the Stephanos boys. If they got a hold of the information, they'd know what she had and would see it coming. They'd be able to block her before she could even get started.

"No." He shook his head. "Someone interrupted my search, and since you don't look like you're about to pass out, I can go ahead and tell you I'm not thrilled with you. You should have told me you heard him coming up the steps. Shut the door, something."

She didn't know what to say. He was right of course, but she couldn't very well tell him that. She wouldn't admit she'd been wrong. Not to him. Her father had sent him, she reminded herself. She couldn't really trust him. Yet, the way he held her, had run after her didn't seem to fit with the other men her father had corralled himself with.

"I have to go back up there." Deciding to ignore the exasperated look in his eyes, she turned toward the stairs.

"No, you need to get in the car so we can get out of here." He grabbed hold of her elbow, stilling her on the steps.

"I need that folder more than you need to bring me back to Chicago. If you are going to take me back there, then I really need it."

His eyes narrowed. "What's in it?"

She couldn't trust him, but at the same time she needed to. "Evidence against my father." She pinched the bridge of her nose, wondering for the hundredth time how her life had gotten so turned upside down. "He killed my fiancé."

4

A simple pickup and return. That's what he'd been sent on, but now he had a colossal mess on his hands. He should have gone with his gut and told Cowsky to get another man, insisted that he be left out of this muck. But his commander knew him enough to know dangling a woman in distress in front of him would be enough to get him moving. Insinuating corrupt cops would make the situation worse had plucked just the right string to make him dance to Cowsky's tune.

Addison St. Claire was not some spoiled little rich kid who'd thrown a temper tantrum and run away. No. She was a grown-ass woman who feared for her life.

His head was starting to hurt.

"What did you say?" It was his turn to take a calming breath. They'd been there too long, they needed to get moving, but her little statement had thrown him.

"A year ago, my father had my fiancé murdered. It was all set up like some car accident, but it wasn't. I have proof."

A car accident. Maybe it really had been and she couldn't cope and blamed Daddy. The conviction in her voice, the steadiness of her stance when she made her accusations though, they spoke of something else. Something less than denial and more of assurance.

The meow of a cat off in the field got him moving again. "We'll talk about it in the car." He tried to grab her again, but she leaped up onto the steps and took them two at a time back into the apartment. Where the, hopefully, dead guy lay.

"Fuck." He chased after her for the third time that night and made it to the door just as she leaned over the limp body, tucking her hair back so as not to touch any of the blood or otherwise. "I'll check him. You get that damn folder," he ordered her when she just kept staring at the body.

Dark blood had saturated the man's brown hair, but didn't pool onto the floor. Head wounds bled like a bitch. The vase lay scattered on the floor beside him, the base of it still in one piece. With his foot, he nudged it, sturdy and thick; no wonder she'd split his head open with it.

"Now, Addison. Get your shit so we can go."

When she still stared down at the silent body, he stepped over the asshole and gripped her shoulders. "Go." Spinning her to face the bedroom door, he sent her away with a hard swat to her ass. Her perfectly plump ass that he refused to think about. He had a much bigger fish to fry at the moment other than how much he had just enjoyed that little slap to her backside, but he'd come back to it later. When he had time to admire and linger over the image.

Her hand reached behind her to cover her bottom, but she scurried away from him, not looking back. He already knew she was a bottom from what he'd been told when given the chore of picking her up, but until that moment, he wasn't positive on how far that submissive side went. Something to explore. Later. After they were far away from her shitty apartment and the half dead Stephanos goon.

Nudging the creep with his foot, he contemplated letting the asshole bleed out. Trevor didn't work organized crime or the drug units, but he'd heard enough to know who was lying on the floor. But, the Boy Scout in him just wouldn't let it go though. He crouched down and felt around the fat neck for a pulse. Weak, and a bit thready, but it was there. He'd be fine, the bleeding had already slowed enough that Trevor wasn't worried about him dying.

The fucker began to moan, a good sign. Except they were still there.

As he stood to go see what was taking Addison so long, she bounded out of the single bedroom with a duffle bag, stuffed to near ripping the zipper. "What's all that?" He pointed.

"I can't come back here." Her eyes landed on the now moving body. "He's okay?"

"He will be. We need to go. Now." He reached out his hand to grab her bag, but she pulled back.

"Wait. Are you still taking me back to Chicago? I can't go home."

Her knuckles were nearly white from gripping the handles of the bag. When he looked in her eyes he saw the one thing he recognized clearly: raw fear. Not the sort of trepidation that got his cock hard when his little sub was waiting for her comeuppance, but true terror. The sort that burns its image into your brain and doesn't wash away no matter how you try.

"We'll talk about it in the car."

"No. Not until you promise you aren't taking me to Chicago."

A pained groan rose up from the no longer unconscious man. Trevor put himself between Addison and the intruder and glared at her. He wanted to grab her, haul her over his shoulder, and take off, but that would be more like kidnapping than set well with him.

"Addison. If I don't take you to your father, you will be under my authority." He glanced back at the

Stephanos ass before continuing. "That means you'll do what I say, when I say, and how I say. There won't be any backtalk, no second-guessing me, and sure as fuck no secrets. You'll tell me everything you know, show me every bit of evidence you have, and you'll do exactly what I say at all times." He pointed a finger at her, watching her eyes dilate as he spoke.

Well, fuck him. He wasn't trying to turn her on; he was trying to get the point straight in her head. But he made a few mental notes for later.

A quick nod and the deal was sealed. "Fine."

He gave a little laugh. "You really should read the fine print, sweetheart, before you go agreeing to shit." He didn't wait for her ask any questions, he just reached over and pulled the bag out of her hands. "Now get going." Sidestepping her, he watched the goon as she scrambled past him and out the door.

He didn't bother with cleaning up or even shutting the door. The asshole wasn't going to be calling the cops; he'd be sporting a hell of a headache for a while, too.

Trevor followed Addison down the steps and to the car, still watching her hips as they gracefully swayed with her walk. The woman wasn't even trying, but every move she made spoke to him on a carnal level. Even with blood splattered on her, she was fucking hot.

"Get in." He pointed to her door as he rounded the

car to put the bag in the trunk. When she tried to stop him and grab the bag, he gave her a heated look. "Get. In. The. Car." Her mouth opened, ready to give him a smartass remark, but she must have remembered the promise she'd just made and snapped it shut again. Good. He needed to figure out what the fuck to do with her now, and her yammering wasn't going to help.

He waited until she was tucked back in her seat before opening the trunk and depositing the bag inside. He could just open it then, dig around and see what she had, but that would be too easy. No, she would show him. She'd lay out everything and show him, and he would either let her keep it, or he'd take it.

Fuck, he was turning into a dirty monster. Something in her was drawing out his darker side, the part of him he kept reserved for the girls in the club when he needed to blow off some steam.

He watched her through the rear window, at the back of her head as she looked down into her lap. Her phone. He'd need to get a look at that, too. After she finished telling him what a shit show he'd been dragged into.

Running his palm over the back of his neck, he resolved himself to his course. Once his decision was made, it was done. Now he just needed to figure out how to execute it.

First thing he needed was to get them someplace to wash up and sleep. Whatever he was going to find when they got settled would determine how long of a night he was going to have.

SHE'S ALMOST KILLED TONY. That knock to his head could have killed him, might have done so if she'd had another inch to her height. When she'd come back out from the bedroom with her things in tow, she'd taken a good look at his face before Trevor blocked her view. Tony. Carmine had sent his coked-out nephew after her. It was probably the only reason she'd been able to get to him before he'd seen her. He had been too high to do the job right. That didn't mean the next guy would be the same.

Taking stock of her evening, her body clenched in the seat beside Trevor. Too quickly she'd gone from managing a strip/sex club to being hauled out of the club and on the run. Would the Stephanos cousins have hurt her? Killed her maybe? Probably. If they had seen what she had in her file, they'd deem her too risky to keep around.

But they didn't have it, didn't know exactly what she had and she wasn't going to just hand it over. It was the only thing keeping her alive at the moment. She wasn't stupid. Her father hadn't sent Trevor to rescue her or to bring his baby girl home. He wanted the file just as badly as the Stephanos family did. She had enough to hurt them both. Keeping it was the only way to assure she'd get out of this mess. She was on her own. She couldn't trust anyone. Not even the cop silently driving his sedan down the darkened highway.

He hadn't said much since he got back in the car at her apartment. Barked at her to buckle herself up, but that was about it. No questions, no checking to be sure she was okay. Nothing. Then again, he was just an overpaid security guard sent to do her father's bidding, right? He might have agreed not to take her back to Chicago right away, but that didn't mean he wouldn't do it anyway. He'd want to know what was in her file, but she'd have to keep some of it to herself. No sense giving it all to him. Not until she knew she could trust him, until she was sure he wasn't a paid mercenary for her father.

He didn't look like one of his father's men. She studied him as he stared out at the road stretched out in front of them. Square jaw, serious expression, ruffled hair. He'd been dragging his hands through it every couple of miles. Either she made him nervous or he was pissed; she couldn't really tell which.

"Where are we going?" she asked when he veered off the highway.

"You need some sleep," he said.

Sleep? It was barely after midnight. Her shifts rarely ended before two in the morning.

"I'm okay. I can drive if you need to sleep." She shifted in her seat, pulling the seat buckle from her chest and rearranging it so it would stop choking her.

He huffed. "No."

She wanted to argue, but his hands clenched around the steering wheel harder. Whatever was eating at him wasn't going to improve by annoying him further.

She sighed and turned away from him, watching the neon lights of a few motels pass them before he finally pulled into a parking lot. He'd skipped all the questionable-looking motels and took them to a Motel 6. Not the Four Seasons, but she'd be fine. She'd been living in a hellhole since moving to the small-ass town, figuring her father wouldn't bother looking for her in that part of town.

With the car parked, he cut the engine, turning to her and giving her a long stare. "I'm going to check us in. You'll be a good girl and stay here, right? No running off or anything like that?" He rested his arm on her head rest. His fingers toyed with a lock of her hair, reminding her how easily a simple touch could soften her edges.

"I'm not going anywhere, Trevor." She used the name she'd seen on his badge to assure him she'd stay put. How helpful could he be if she ran away? No, until she knew more about him, she'd just stick it out. He couldn't be worse than her father, and if she'd managed to survive his threats and his insults for her entire life, she could handle a little glaring from Trevor.

His eyes wandered over her face, as though he was trying to detect dishonesty from her. He'd have to keep looking, that wasn't her game. Lying, cheating, embezzling, laundering, extortion—that was her father's racket, not hers.

He moved his hand from her hair to trail his fingertips down her jaw, stopping at her chin and grasping it. "I'll be right back."

The spot where he'd touched her, held onto her, tingled once his touch was gone. She blinked when the car door slammed and watched him saunter off toward the office. His t-shirt was tucked into his jeans, giving her a good view of his physique. She'd already taken in his broad shoulders and thick muscular arms, but seeing his thighs and ass as he moved put the whole deal together. Definitely something she could sink her teeth into.

She shook her head. It had been too long since she'd been with a man. That had to be why she was coveting his ass like some prized ham. Her last sexual encounter with a man had been with Steven. The night before he was killed. If she let the memory come to her, she'd remember the snap of the dragon tail, the bite of every stroke he gave her, and the mind-melting orgasm that followed. But she wouldn't let that memory surface. She hadn't in a long time. Steven was gone, never returning, and no number of tears or wishing would change that fact. Dwelling on what she'd lost wouldn't get her anywhere. She needed to focus on the future.

"Okay, we're here." Her car door popped open, scaring her until she recognized Trevor's voice. "Whoa, do you always startle so easy?" he laughed.

She released the seatbelt and pushed herself out of the car. "No," she snapped and rounded the car to the trunk. "I need my bag." She tapped the trunk.

He closed her door, keeping his eyes on her the entire time and walked over to her. His lips were loose, not quite forming a grin, but no longer tense in growl formation either. "Ask nicely."

She stared at him. It was late, it was chilly, and now after having to deal with him and everything else, getting some sleep actually sounded like a good plan.

"I'm waiting." He crossed his arms over his chest and leaned one hip against the trunk of the car.

She exhaled her impatience and fought the urge to stomp her foot. She may have been a little pampered growing up, but bratting wasn't her style. "Will you please get my bag?" She said the right words, but even she could hear the sarcasm dripping from each syllable.

He shook his head and tsked. "Try again, princess."

"I really hate that name. It doesn't even fit."

"Noted. Now, try again."

She could try to out-wait him, but by the carefree expression he had she doubted he would care. Besides he had the key to the car and the motel room.

"Will you please open the trunk so I can get my bag?"

For a long moment, he didn't say anything, just stared at her, then the corner of his mouth upturned and he cracked a smile. "There. That wasn't so bad, was it, sweet-cheeks?" He patted her cheek and pulled the keys from his pocket.

The trunk popped open before she could comment on the new nickname he'd given her and he'd grabbed the bag.

"I can carry it." She reached for it but he'd already turned away and shut the trunk.

"This way, sweet-cheeks."

That name was even worse. She scowled at his back but followed him to their room, which was right in front of where he had parked. His doing and not some coincidence, she was sure.

When she caught up with him, the door was already open. She brushed past him, feeling his heat as she did so and took in the room. One bed.

"We need another room." She turned toward the door.

He shut the door and slid the chain lock. "Why?" He was still holding her bag in his hand.

"There's only one bed." She pointed to the queen bed, not even a king.

"So?" A dark eyebrow rose, he didn't even look at the room; he just kept his gaze on her.

She sighed. "Fine. Whatever, sleep on the floor, what do I care?" She made a grab for the duffle, but he clamped his hand around her arm before she even touched it.

"Rules, Addison. Let's go over them now so we don't have any misunderstandings. Rule number one. You don't tell me shit. You may ask me, you may suggest, but you don't tell me anything."

His fingers bit into her arm, and trying to twist out of his grip only resulted in more pain. Giving up, she resigned herself to go along with him. For now, anyway.

"Okay. Okay, Trevor." She yanked her arm back when he loosened his grip. "Can I please have my bag." She held her out her hand, not looking at him at all.

"No. I want to see what's inside. Sit over there." He pointed to the one armchair in the corner of the room, a dimly lit reading lamp burned behind it.

"See what's inside? Just my clothes and the folder." She tried again to reach for it, but again he was quick to grab her. This time though, he didn't just hold onto her, he spun her around, pinning her arm behind her back. Hot pain soared through her shoulder as he pulled her hand a little higher. He pushed her the few steps to the bed and shoved her down onto it.

Her face buried in the coral-colored bedspread, she had to turn her head to get air. He pressed down on her, his body pinning her to the bed.

"Like I said earlier. No backtalk. No disobeying. I said I wanted to see what's inside. So, I'm going to look." She could feel him touching her. His body covered her own, his lips only a few inches from her ear as he spoke.

"Okay. Okay! You're hurting me, Trevor." She pushed back, but he only pinned her harder.

"Go sit in that chair and don't say another word." He pulled her back to her feet and released her. Her hair was disheveled, covering her face from being tossed around like a ragdoll. Wiping it out of her face, she went to the chair and eased into it. She rubbed her shoulder, trying to get the burn out.

"You want tell me what I'll find?" He plopped the bag on the bed and unzipped it.

"I already told you. Just my clothes and the folder." She ground her teeth together. Would he be angry when he found out she was lying?

5

Most people had a tell when they were lying. He could almost always spot it given enough time with the person. Some would clear their throat right before they lied, others would nibble their lip. Addison's ears turned red. Bright crimson from earlobe to ear tip. It was cute, adorable really, and totally out of her control.

"Remember I did say no lying. No secrets." He watched for another minute as she squirmed, her ears burning red, but she made no attempt to correct her statement. He sighed, almost disappointed. "Okay."

Opening the duffle further, he saw what she had said, clothes. Taking each piece out one at a time, he looked them over, enjoying her growing discomfort more than someone in his position really should. A sweater, a t-shirt, two pairs of jeans. Then he got to the good stuff. Panties. He made sure to hold them up and get a good look. Satin, not the fake shit you see in department stores, but real satin and lace panties that left very little to the imagination once they were on. And of course, matching bras. She wasn't looking at him anymore; her red face was turned away.

He should feel bad. The woman was having a bad time of it, and there he was playing with her panties. Well, tough. He wasn't in the mood for any more fucking surprises and since she wasn't going to spill all the dirt, he had to get the information another way.

Underneath the clothes, he found a hairbrush, some makeup, and then a cigar box on top of a manila file folder. He glanced back over at her, noting the initial worry, and pulled the cigar box out. Heavy.

As he shuffled the box, the contents moved. He knew that sound, that weight. "What's in here, Addison?" he asked, holding up the cigar box.

She licked her lips and shrugged one shoulder. Silence really wasn't the correct answer, but she'd figure that out soon enough. "I'll ask again, Addison, but this is the last time I'm going to repeat myself. What's in here?"

"My gun." She brought her eyes to his, raising her chin as she gave him what he wanted to know. Her defiance only worked to arouse him more, and he didn't want to be aroused. Not by her.

"And why the hell do you have a gun?" He flipped

the lid open on the box and removed the revolver. An antique by the looks of it. He closed his eyes to take a deep breath. She was an intelligent woman by all accounts, why the fuck would she think an antique gun would be an acceptable form of protection?

"Why do you?" she shot back at him, raising her chin just a little more.

"Because I'm a police officer." He tossed the box on the bed, keeping the gun in his hand while he turned to her, closing in on her quickly. "This thing is so old it would probably backfire and hit you instead. Have you ever even shot a gun before, Addison?"

Of course she hadn't, and the look on her face when he asked the question confirmed it. Why would the daughter of Jacob St. Claire need to know how to fire a gun? He flicked open the chamber and the heat on his neck grew.

"Did you load this yourself?" He carefully closed it back up, and put the safety on. He looked over the Smith & Wesson Victory model in his hand with some admiration mixed with anger. Not much of a gun buff himself, but he was a WWII history fanatic. The gun he held in his hands was released in 1942 and had been carried as a sidearm by the soldiers of the Second World War.

"It's loaded?" she asked.

If she hadn't been grinning like a cat mid-meal of canary, he might have lost his temper.

"Of course I loaded it. I know how to shoot it." That was a lie. She may have loaded it, but no way on earth she could shoot it.

"Okay, come here." He crooked a finger at her. With some hesitation, she meandered to him, her eyes never leaving the revolver he held in his hand. The excitement of holding such an authentic piece of history was dampened by where it came from and who it belonged to. "Is this your father's?"

"Of course it is." She rolled her eyes. Actually rolled them. Few things irritated him more in a woman than rolling her eyes like a schoolgirl. It was disrespectful and juvenile.

"So, you stole it, loaded it, and intended on doing what? You didn't even have it with you at work. You left it at home, buried somewhere?"

She huffed. "My father—he has connections, obviously. You know that, seeing as you're here trying to take me back to him. I mean you're a fucking cop. I'm over eighteen; if I don't want to live at home anymore you can't do anything about that. I'm twenty-four, for Christ's sake! So, as you can see, he's connected. I knew he wouldn't like that I left, and the Stephanos family sure as hell wouldn't like it either. I needed protection." She eyed the revolver.

"I need to know everything, Addison. From start to finish." He picked up the cigar box again, flipped the gun's cartridge open and dumped the bullets out, before stowing it away.

She watched him, and he could see turmoil brewing. She wasn't wrong in her assessment. He had been sent to drag her back home, kicking and screaming. Being of legal age, and having broken no laws, and Michigan being completely out of his jurisdiction, he had no right to be doing it, yet here he was. What had started out trying to do the right thing for his commander had quickly turned into something much larger. Something more important.

"I don't trust you." The softly spoken words bit at him. No reason they should, but they did just the same.

"Well, I'm sorry about that, but it doesn't matter. I can't protect you if I don't know what I'm protecting you from."

"I just wanted to be left alone. I didn't want anyone to come for me, and I don't want to go home," she said. The hitch in her voice struck him. It had been a long day for her, and it wasn't going to be getting any easier going forward.

"Did you take cash?" The memory of the beaten-up hole in the wall she'd been living in entered his mind. No one of her social stature would live like that if they didn't absolutely have to.

"Of course I did, but not his money. Mine. It's

mine, but I hadn't touched it until last week. There was a payroll issue, and I needed cash."

That's how he'd found her. It was easy to track a bank withdrawal. That would give her father a town, and it probably didn't take much longer to figure out where she was working.

"This folder." He paused to pick up the manila folder from the duffle. "Is this what they're looking for?"

Her eyes widened and she started to reach for it, but he pulled it out of her reach.

"It's mine!" she yelled and lunged for it.

He held her at bay with a hand to her chest, just above her breasts. Her heart beat hard beneath his touch. "Calm down, Addison." He splayed his fingers wider, pushing her back just enough for her to understand. He wasn't just bigger and stronger than her; he was in control of the situation.

Her eyes flashed to his. "How do I know you weren't sent to keep me quiet?" She stepped back; his hand dropped to his side. "How do I know Daddy didn't send you to shut me up? To make me play nice?" Another step back, toward the door now.

"Addison." She actually thought her own father would send someone to kill her? To do horrible things to her to make her play his game? Well, why not? It wasn't as though he hadn't seen worse than that in his missing persons cases.

"Well? How can I be sure?" she demanded with more force than a woman in her position really should be allowed, but he wasn't going to push those buttons. Not yet anyway.

"Your father asked the department to have someone bring you home. That's it, nothing else, nothing more." His assurance wasn't getting him very far. Her eyes narrowed, but at least her breathing started to slow, become more that of a reasonable person. "I swear it."

He sat down on the bed, hoping the space would give her some comfort. He didn't want her bolting from the room, and not just because he didn't feel up to chasing her. He didn't want her to get herself hurt. And a woman like her, with no actual knowledge of the streets would get hurt, or killed. The Stephanos brothers, or her father, would find her. Either way, she didn't have much of a chance without him. But he still needed to know exactly why they were after her. What made her run away from home?

"It would be better if I just went off on my own."

"No, it would be easier for me, but not better." It wouldn't be easy to let her walk out of the motel and fend for herself, he'd lied about that. He'd worry. He wouldn't want to, but he would all the same. "Look. Go take a shower. While you're doing that, I'll read through this file and when you're done we can talk."

"I don't—"

"Take your shower, Addison. We'll talk when you're done." He scooted back on the bed, resting against the headboard and cradling the folder on his lap.

She hesitated another moment more, then grabbed her clothes from the mussed-up pile on the bed and stomped off to the bathroom, slamming the door behind her.

Once he heard the water running, he settled in, kicking off his boots and opening the thick file. She'd been thorough if nothing else.

"Now to see what the fuck has her on the run."

THE LIGHTS CRACKLED as the bulbs burned in the bathroom while Addison waited for the water to warm up. Overall the motel wasn't horrible. The tub appeared clean, the floor wasn't sticking to her shoes, and the mirror had been wiped down. Hell of a lot better than the bathroom at Boom Boom.

She took a quick look at her reflection, then decided to leave it to chance. Her makeup was smeared, she knew that already, and her hair looked more like a bird's nest than a head of hair, and she didn't want to see it. Up until a few hours ago, everything had been going okay. Not wonderful. She was a manager of a strip/kink club and not the middle school English teacher she wanted to be, but she was free. Her father wasn't hanging over her shoulder with his agenda and his orders and Jesse Stephanos wasn't being shoved at her every chance her father had.

Travel bottles of generic shampoo and conditioner were in the stall. The perfumes would probably make her skin itch, but she had no other choice. Her father never understood the sensitivities she had to fragrances. Every year he'd buy her a new lot of perfumes, and get red-faced pissed when she declined to wear them. Between the dry patches and scaly skin most fragrances inflicted upon her, she wasn't adventurous when it came to perfume, but she needed to clean some of the sweat away from her hair. That run though the field near her apartment had been the most exercise she'd gotten since she left Chicago.

Hot water quickly turned cold, and she hurried with the small bar of soap, cleaning off her skin as best she could. When she dried off and the skin on her arms began to tighten, she knew she'd be spending the whole night scratching.

Once she'd squeezed as much water from her hair she could, she wiggled her way into a pair of leggings and a t-shirt. She assumed he'd let her sleep, and she wasn't in the habit of sleeping in her jeans.

As she opened the bathroom door, a cool breeze blew in at her from the room. She found him just as she'd left him. Lying casually on the bed, folder in his lap. Though his brow was more furrowed, his jaw firmer as he read the pages of her file. He'd shucked off his boots and socks at some point, his bare feet crossed at the ankle. He'd even removed his shirt.

She swallowed. Dear God. His chest was massive. All solid muscle from what she could tell, and a large tattoo covered his right pec. An intricate design that she couldn't place, but the feeling that it had a deeper meaning for him overwhelmed her.

He must have noticed her staring at him and he lifted his chin to see her. Realizing her jaw had fallen open, she snapped her mouth shut. He noticed of course, and the arrogant grin she'd seen earlier at the club returned.

"It was hot, hope you don't mind, I turned the air on."

She heard the rattling of the wall unit shoved beneath the window of the room. "N-no, it's fine." She carried her dirty clothes to the duffle bag and went about reorganizing her things.

"Your fiancé." He started to talk as she zipped the bag closed. "Why did your father want him out of the picture?"

"We were going to move out of state after the wedding. Steven's from Minnesota originally and we were going to move up there." She took a deep breath. "Daddy didn't want me leaving the city much less the state. He kept pressuring me to leave Steven. And when I wouldn't—" A year had passed and still she had a hard time saying the words out loud. "He had him killed." Turning away, she dropped the bag on the floor near the dresser and busied herself with braiding her hair.

When she turned back he was staring at her. Not looking at her, but staring, hard. She realized then the chill had hardened her nipples and the shirt she wore was thinner than she remembered. The light from behind her probably gave him a clear view of everything beneath it.

She moved away, tossing herself into the corner chair and began braiding and unbraiding her hair. "Are you going to help me, or should I just buy a bus ticket?"

He closed the file and stared at her. "How did you get all this?" He jammed a finger at the folder.

"What the hell does that matter?" It hadn't been easy, and more than once she'd barely gotten away without being seen. She may be an English teacher by trade, but Steven was one of the best IT personnel she'd ever met. She hadn't ignored him when he talked, and had spent more than one night curled up at his feet while he tapped away on his computer. She'd learned a few things, and those bits of knowledge came in handy when searching computers and digging up old text messages. Her father wasn't as smart as he thought.

Trevor shook his head. "It doesn't, but I want to know. How did you get this?"

She sighed. Of course he'd want to know everything. He was a fucking cop after all. "I hacked into computers, email servers mostly. For other bits I used a Xerox machine."

"Xerox—" He closed his eyes, snapped them shut really, and took a steadying breath. He did that a lot, she realized. "You snuck into offices and made copies?"

"How else was I supposed to get the stuff that wasn't on the computers?"

"Okay." He pinched the bridge of his nose. "You realized how dangerous that was, right? I mean you knew it and did it anyway?"

She didn't see what that mattered, but decided to play along with his questions. "Of course I knew it was dangerous. I was digging up information on my father's criminal activities. I'm not stupid."

"But you did it anyway." He held up a hand to stop her from answering. "Never mind. Obviously, you did. What were you going to do with all this?"

This part he'd probably get a good laugh at. She'd almost found it funny herself. Her ignorance had almost been her undoing.

"I was going to hand it over to the police. I had a meeting set up with a detective, but it didn't happen." She started braiding her hair again.

He watched her fingers while they worked. "Why?"

"I realized he was friends with my father. I left town the night he informed Daddy I was meeting with him the next morning."

Trevor took another of his breaths and shoved the file to the side. "So, your father knows you have all this, which means the Stephanoses know you have it, and they both want you back."

"They want the information. I don't think the Stephanos family will want me as an in-law now. They'll see me as a threat."

"Your father."

"Don't you think it's weird that he sent you, and then the Stephanoses show up?" She unbraided her locks and pulled her knees up to her chest.

"The whole situation is fucked up," he said. "Sending a cop to fetch his daughter? He could have gotten any one of his little goons to do the job, or let the Stephanos family come for you. I don't know what his reasoning is, but I'm sure he has a plan."

"I'm not going back to find out what it is."

"No, you're not," he said. "Is this the only copy?"

"The only hard copy. I scanned them to my Dropbox account," she said, her fingers still working her hair.

"But you carry around the hard copy?" He shook his head.

"I had it ready to hand over to that detective. I probably should have left it behind or shredded it. But does it really matter? I have the information and that's why the Stephanos family is after me, and it's why my father wants me home."

"They aren't going to give up so easily. You can't go back to Chicago yet. Not until it's safe. You'll stay with me until that happens." He scooted to the edge of the bed, dropping his feet down, his knees touching hers.

"What about you? You have a job. If you don't bring me back, won't you get in trouble? I mean doesn't the department track you or something?" She wished she knew about police work, so she didn't sound so naive.

"I'll call my commander in the morning. Technically none of this is official. But, since he's expecting me back by Monday, I'll have to eat into my vacation time. At least then we won't have the Chicago PD breathing down my neck."

"You're going to use vacation time." She laughed. The absurdities were starting to pile up around them. "My father is going to put pressure on the department if he used his influence to get them to send you in the first place."

She was twenty-four years old. She didn't need to explain to him, she just needed to get the hell away from him.

"You're abusing your power," she leaned forward to whisper. "I won't fuck you for your help."

He laughed. "We haven't gotten to that yet, but if

we get there, you'll do it for other reasons. Hell, you'll beg me or it won't happen at all."

Her mouth dried. The conversation had gotten a little off course. "I—what do you think you know about me?" She tilted her head. Her father had a lot of sick twisted ideas as to what she did during her free time. On more than one occasion he'd threatened to have the clubs she frequented with Steven shut down for immoral something or other. He had to have told Trevor. And, it probably didn't help she'd been managing a club that engaged in kink behind curtains.

His hand brushed against her knee. His tongue ran across his bottom lip. "You're not into just scening. You've never played with someone that wasn't more than just your top." Fingertips tapped her knee. "You're a submissive."

She put her hand over his to shove him away, but once her hand was there, once his warmth touched her, she just held onto him. Feeling the strength in his fingers as she wrapped hers around his.

"You can't know that."

"Sure I can." He grinned, that arrogance again.

"How can you know something like that, I've been with you a few hours at most."

"Because I've seen you. At Leather and Lace on Wabash."

6

The resemblance had troubled Trevor since he'd seen her picture in the file he was given. He couldn't place her other than to know he'd seen her somewhere before. Shaking it off as having probably recognized her from a tabloid or newspaper article, he hadn't looked into it any further. Even when he dug into her personal life and found out she frequented the local BDSM club, the little carrot her father used to keep her in line, he hadn't linked the pieces together.

But when he looked up from the file to see her standing in her leggings and shirt, the memory flooded back to him. He'd seen those curvy thighs before, stretched taut as she was bent over a bench, her leggings pulled down, baring her round ass for the crowd. Thick red welts crossed her ass, new ones being added with each strike of the cane her top held. The sound of her cries, those he remembered clearly. A soft moan that quickly grew in intensity until she was nearly growling. It was that sound that had stopped him from just walking by the scene and instead he'd stopped to watch. He'd seen her take a solid caning, heard and loved every grunt and sound uttered from her lips. He'd only managed to walk away when the girl he was meeting arrived.

"Y-you saw me?" She hadn't moved her hand away, he noticed. The soft, warm touch of her skin pressing against his, not quite pushing his away, but not holding him either. "When?"

He pulled his hand from under hers and patted her thigh. "A few times, really, but I didn't know who you were. I didn't recognize you until just now." Some of the embarrassment eased from her eyes, but not completely. He didn't like seeing any. Being a submissive wasn't something to have shame about. Too many women saw it as something to be shoved down into their dark places, misunderstanding completely that it was the darkness he sought in them.

"Don't do that." He sounded angry. He didn't mean to be angry, but the look of unease didn't suit her.

"What?"

He pushed away, standing from the bed and walking across the room. "Looking all embarrassed. So I saw you at a dungeon, with your pants around your ankles and your ass getting caned. You were having a damn good time, and I was fucking loving the scene. There's nothing to be embarrassed about."

Addison sucked in a breath and rested her forehead on her knees. "I'm not embarrassed you saw me, or that I was there." Her chin lifted, and watery eyes met his. "Steven used to take me there. I've only ever been there with him."

Well, fuck. Her fiancé. The one her father supposedly had killed. That's who he'd seen her with? While he was lusting after her, imagining her while he'd played with the lady he'd picked for the night. How could he not have recognized her when he saw her earlier?

"I read your file on him." Knowing what to say in moments of awkward silence had never been his strength. His older brother, Devin, always knew what to say. But not him; the years working on missing persons didn't help. Having to tell a sobbing mother she'd never see her little boy again never got easier. He hadn't been able to harden himself to those tears. He blamed his brother for that. Devin had always been his protector. Keeping him from seeing the shit that little kids shouldn't see. And as they got older, he kept him from knowing shit he didn't need to know.

Until their mother was killed. Devin couldn't protect him from that.

Addison blinked and caught a single tear with the

flat of her thumb before it rolled down her cheek. "What did you think?" She dropped her feet to the floor and rubbed her palms across her thighs.

"Well." He reached over the bed and picked up the folder, flipping through it again. He didn't need to; he'd nearly memorized it all already. The woman took long showers, and he had a strong memory. She'd done good detective work.

"There seems to be enough leads to start digging around. There's more than just your fiancé's murder in here though. Direct evidence about your father." He understood wanting the truth about her fiancé, but that death had included the Stephanos family, as well as many of the dealings her father had had outside that one incidence. Going to the cops with as much as she had could blow open an entire case against the Stephanos family. A Rico case, that would drag her father into the fold. For something like that, the Stephanos family surely wanted her dead, and her father, maybe him too.

"I know. I'm the one who put it all together."

He didn't care for the snark in her voice, but he'd let it slip. For now.

"Exactly how did you get all this?" he demanded to know. Some of the evidence included photographs of ledgers, secret files, computer printouts—one didn't get those things by just asking for them.

"I already told you. I went and got them. What's

the next step? Don't you have someone at the precinct you can call, get us a meeting or something?" The hope in her voice was almost painful.

She had no idea how the PD worked. "There isn't exactly an app on my phone that reads Organized Crime and Killer Daddy." He regretted his tone when her eyes hardened. A stubborn Addison wouldn't get them very far. "I work missing persons, Addison. I have very little contact outside my department." For good reason, too. "And for something like this, something that involves your father and the Stephanos family, we need to be sure we can trust who we take this to."

She nodded. "That detective I was going to meet, he turned out to be friends with my father."

The system was corrupt and full of old cronies who knew how to manipulate it. Even a file folder full of evidence wouldn't work unless they found someone in the PD that wouldn't hand it off to her father and tip off the Stephanos family.

"I'll figure out something, but until then we stay out of Chicago and lay low." He tossed the folder onto the nightstand, the cheap compressed wood shaking from the weight and making the lamp rattle.

"Thank you."

He ran his fingers through his hair. "You may want to hold onto the gratitude until this is all over." He plopped down on the bed, folding his hands behind his head and watching her fidget in her chair. She didn't know what the hell to do with herself. "Addison. Turn off that lamp and get in bed. You need some rest, and I need the quiet."

"Where will you sleep?" She took a hesitant step toward the bed.

He blew out some air. "Right here. I'm not going to hurt you. I won't do anything unless you beg. Then maybe, just maybe I'll give you something. But I'm not in the habit of taking what's not given."

A soft reddening of her cheeks made his dick hard again. He'd finally gotten rid of the image of her bent over with those fucking stripes all over her ass, and now she went and got him all aroused again. "Get in the bed, Addison."

She sucked in her bottom lip then shuffled around the bed, pulling the bedspread and sheet back and jumping in. He reached over to turn off the lamp she'd forgotten and when he turned back to her, the blankets were pulled up to her chin and she had her eyes clamped shut. Just her fingertips were showing outside the covers. Adorable and arousing at the same time.

"My father's not going to like you helping me," she pointed out into the darkness.

He smiled, sure she couldn't see it with her eyes still closed. "No, he's not." And he didn't give a fuck. It was because of men like him, like the Stephanos assholes, that people like his mother hadn't lived to see their grandkids born. No loose strings. That mentality had gotten her killed.

"I'm not ashamed of being a submissive." The whispered confession filled the space between them. He didn't move, just listened as she continued. "I mean, I used to be, not ashamed, just shy about it. It wasn't like that with Steven though. He loved being a dom—my dom. He never let me hide who I was. I mean he didn't walk me down the street in a collar and leash or anything." She giggled. A light sound he wanted to hear more of. "But he was just him, always, and he expected the same from me."

"Your dad threatened him before his death?" Stick to the facts, the best way to handle a case. Don't get too attached, and sure as hell don't pull her into your arms and hold her, like his body begged him to do.

"He threatened a lot of things. He threatened to have the club shut down if I didn't stop going there, arresting the owner, charging members for sexual misconduct or something. I don't know, but it was all just a way for him to control me. To make me do what he wanted. After Steven died, he got his way on that."

Trevor slid his body down the bed, nestling up against her body but not going under the covers. He meant what he said. He didn't take what wasn't given, and even though he could feel her body heat, could sense she was needing a release, he wouldn't touch her.

"When I told my father that I'd never break up with Steven, he had him killed." Her voice shook, a long festering anger lurking in her words. "And he just got away with it, with everything."

"It's going to be okay, Addison. I won't let him or those Stephanos creeps come after you. Just get some sleep now."

Through the darkness, he made out her silhouette; she nodded and wiggled further beneath the covers. He turned to his side, keeping her as close to him as he could with the blankets between them and tried to wipe out the image of her bent over that spanking bench.

"I hate the fucking cane, by the way," she whispered. "Steven only used it when he was punishing me. So, if that's what you saw, that's what he was doing."

What the hell was he supposed to say to that?

"Addison." He took a calming breath and closed his eyes, not wanting to make out the curve of her breasts beneath the covers, or hear her soft breathing. "Go to sleep."

"If you were there, that means... you're a dominant?"

"Sleep. Now." He inched closer to her.

"Just a top?"

He threw his hand over her midsection, pulling her to his body and nuzzling closer to her hair. The motel shampoo was heavily scented. It didn't seem to fit on her. "Sleep."

"You're not embarrassed, are you?" The challenge in her voice poked his dominant side. She was teasing him. Could she be coaxing him into topping her, at that moment?

"No, I'm not. I'm tired. And if you don't shut your mouth and go to sleep, you'll see how *not* embarrassed I am." As a threat, it wasn't much of one.

"Will you spank me, if I'm naughty?"

HAD she really just asked that? Would he spank her? What the hell was she thinking?

All that talk about Steven being her dominant, the club where they played, and the knowledge that Trevor had actually witnessed one of her punishments had her submissive juices flowing again. They had been dried up for so long at first, she didn't recognize what she was up to.

She was bratting. And she didn't brat.

"If I spank you, will you shut up and sleep?"

A pity spanking? "It was a joke, asshole." The blankets tightened around her as she twisted to her side, facing away from him. His heavy arm just pulled her closer to him, cradling her to his body.

"It's late, and I've had a really shitty day, and you

are being a brat. Go to bed. This is your last warning. You'll hate my belt as much as you hate the cane, trust me on that. Go to sleep." His breath was hot against her ear, his arm clamped around her even tighter, nearly pressing the air from her lungs.

"I was just kidding," she whispered, closing her eyes and trying to pretend his rejection didn't sting. What had she been thinking? A little spanking would help her tension? Or did she just want his hands, those large, thick hands on her bare ass, caressing and kneading her until he spanked her red?

"Well, I'm not." He nuzzled her hair with his nose. "No more talking."

She took a few steady breaths, trying to find a way back to where she'd left her pride, sure she'd come up with something to fix the conversation. To take back what she'd asked for, what she wanted from him. Nothing came.

After an hour of lying in the dark, listening to his even breathing, she shoved the covers off and went in search of her phone. Maybe a few minutes on Facebook would get her mind off of things, and she could sleep.

She dug out her phone from her purse and opened the app. A picture of a half-naked man with a completely nude woman kneeling before him lit up the screen. She examined the woman's face. Serene, content, proud. The man's strong hand was in her hair, gripping it behind her in ponytail fashion, pulling her head back to force her eyes up at him. Her throat, elongated from the position, had another of his hands around it.

What would Trevor's hand feel like around her throat? Would he cut off her air, or just hold her there, letting the threat linger and entice her? Maybe just squeeze enough to make her fear come to the surface.

She sank down into the chair in the corner, and clicked on the post. Several more photographs popped up. Scrolling through them, she imagined having Trevor touch her, doing the things she saw in the post. She knew it was wrong. He was a cop. He was only doing his job by helping her. But that didn't stop her from fantasizing, feeling his hands on her.

"What are you doing?" His voice could have been ice water pouring over her. She froze. "Addison. What are you doing?" She knew that voice, what that tone meant.

The bed creaked as he stood and took the few steps toward her. She pressed the button on the side of her phone to make the screen black out, but he only swiped it back to life when he took it. She really needed to put a password on her phone. The glow of the screen allowed her to see the sleepy look on his face, and then his left eyebrow arch.

"Having fun, were you?" He looked down at her lap.

When had her hand slipped into her pants? Oh, god, she'd been touching herself. Was she that hard up, that she was now masturbating unconsciously and with a stranger lying only feet away? She yanked her hand out and tried to snatch her phone from him, but he only tsked his tongue and sat on the bed, scrolling through the same images she just had.

"Give me that." She leapt from the chair and tried again to get from him, but he was faster, and had much more skill. She found herself face down on the bed again, one arm pinned behind her, his pelvis pushing against her ass. She could feel his erection poking at her, and the need to have his touch compounded.

"Which of these was your favorite?" He put the phone in front of her face, scrolling through the pictures with his thumb. Couldn't he just leave it alone? It was bad enough he'd caught her looking at them with her hands in her damn pants; did he really need to rub her nose in it as well?

"Let me up." She turned her head away, refusing to play his game. But her defiance didn't feel right. She wasn't fully invested in making him let her up. Did she want him to make her answer him?

"Not yet." He pressed a knee to her back and read-justed his stance so he had a better position with the phone. "I like this one. Look, Addison."

When she turned back, obeying his command

without hesitation, she took in the photograph. A woman, on her knees facing the man in the picture. Her dark hair was wound around his fist, being pulled backward to make her look up at him. His lips just barely touching hers, not really touching at all really, just hovering right over her. The desire in her expression was unmistakable, the want and need portrayed perfectly. It was one of her favorites as well.

"See how much she wants him, how much she craves his kiss? He's completely in control, he may or may not give her what she wants, and that's what she needs, isn't it, Addison? She needs him to hold that authority?" He'd leaned down when he spoke, his breath brushing her cheek, and his back pressing her into the bed. "It's what you need, too." His lips brushed against her skin, with a softness that should not have held such power behind it, but it did. "You need some relief I think, from the stressful day, from the terrible year you've had?" He let go of her wrist and grabbed the waistband of her leggings.

She should have tried to wiggle free, to get away from him, or at least tell him to stop. Instead, she found herself lifting her hips from the bed to make it easier for him. He chuckled a little at her cooperation as he pushed the leggings down over her ass and went back for her panties.

"I'll give you a choice, Addison. You can fuck yourself with your fingers, like this, bent over the bed and me behind you, watching. Or I can do it for you. You're going to come hard, that's not your choice. Your choice is only who will give it to you."

Just his words were enough to awaken every ounce of her libido, but the smell of him so close, the feel of his fingertips as they traced the curve of her ass, damn near melted her. She hadn't had a man touch her since Steven, but she hadn't wanted to either.

"Fuck, your ass is even more spankable than I thought." He patted her cheeks and her face heated at the mental image of her backside bouncing. Body image wasn't an issue, but she wasn't stupid either. She held a little more curvature than most women found comfortable, and probably most men as well. A sharp slap to her right cheek had her bucking up. "What's your decision, Addison?"

"You don't get to just slap me and do this because I'm. Well. Because I was submissive to my fiancé!" Finally, the logical side of her brain showed up to the party, over ruling her entirely too aroused body's decision to let him continue handling her.

To her surprise, his knee disappeared from her back, his entire body moved from her, leaving her chilled. The bed creaked and when she looked over her shoulder, she saw him standing a few feet behind her.

"You're right." He nodded. "I don't get to just do that." Sincerity hung in his voice, though he looked torn by his own decision. "Do you want me to pull up your panties and tuck you back into bed?"

Alarms should have rung through her body. The lingering disappointment that he'd backed off so easily should not have weighed on her so heavily. Yet, there it was. She was almost angry at him for just giving up.

"You brought up consent, Addison. So, you'll either have to tell me you want this, want me to step up here, or you'll have to pull up your panties and get in bed."

The situation had changed too quickly, like a tornado had just blown through and turned everything upside down. He wanted her to consent to him topping her, dominating her?

She just laid there, her naked ass facing him, her pussy clamping down in desire, and her mind working overtime to put everything together. To come up with a way out of the mess she had made of the moment. One thing she knew for certain, she wanted his hands back on her. She wanted to have that feeling of being overpowered, protected, and she hadn't had that feeling in a long time.

But to say it out loud was another thing entirely.

"Addison, I'm gonna lay this out for you really easy. I don't play nice. I don't allow disobedience, disrespect, or bad behavior of any kind. When I ask a question, I expect it answered. When I give you a choice, and that will be a rare occurrence, you have to make a fucking choice. So, what's it going to be?"

Pushing up from the bed, she turned to face him. Her panties and leggings were stuck around her knees, and her shirt covered most of her, yet the vulnerability rolling through her had little to do with her state of undress. He leaned one hip against the table and crossed his arms over his chest. He wouldn't be making a move until she did, that much was pretty damn clear.

"You won't take me back to Chicago? You'll help me?"

"I already said I would." He nodded but sounded irritated. She hadn't meant to question his integrity if that's what he was thinking.

Addison bent over, keeping her eyes on his face. She didn't meet his gaze, no, she wasn't ready for that yet. She focused on a spot on his chin, hoping to at least give the appearance that she was looking directly at him, and shoved her panties and pants to the floor, stepping out of them. Deciding to go all in, she gathered the hem of her shirt in her hand, tore it over her head, and tossed it on the bed.

Fighting the urge to cover herself even after taking the steps to bare herself, she put her fisted hands at her sides, raised her chin, and brought her eyes as close to his as she could manage. "Fine, then."

7

She was adorable, thinking she only needed to say two words and everything would just start up and go from there. Obviously, she wanted that release, that orgasm he was promising her, but he wanted more. A hell of a lot more. And it made no fucking sense to him.

At some point in the past few hours the woman had gone from being his target to his capture and now she was his to shield. Not just that, no, that would be too easy, now he was making her his. Really his. At least for the time they had together. Before it all either went to complete shit, and he either got them both killed or he actually managed to get through the corruption and bureaucracy of the PD to find some actual justice.

She stared at him, those large brown eyes of hers

fixated on his chin. She could hide for the time being, but it wouldn't last long. Addison wasn't shy about her submissiveness, at least not since he'd called her out on it and made her confront it.

He hadn't asked her to take off her shirt, but he figured she was trying to make some sort of symbolic gesture. She'd learn in time to do what she was told, and nothing more. What if he had wanted to remove the shirt himself? She'd just stolen that from him.

Once she started to fidget beneath his stare, he started to take in all of her. Now that she was fully nude, he could see everything. Every wonderful curve, every sensual place he wanted to kiss and nibble, and every flaw that made her fucking gorgeous. He made it perfectly clear he was looking her over, inclining his head this way and that as his gaze moved lower. A tiny patch of dirty blonde hair covered a small area just above her mons. Neatly trimmed and well groomed. Two swipes of a razor and the patch would be gone, but it wouldn't be by his command.

"Turn," he said while twirling his finger in the air. She looked ready to argue, it was there on the tip of her tongue ready to jump out, but she pressed her lips together hard and straightened her arms at her sides. As she made the little turn, he took in the small curve of her belly, her delicious thighs—those thighs he wanted to get between more and more as the moments ticked by. If he didn't do something about his own needs pretty soon there was going to be more than just a wet spot on his pants.

When she'd made it back around to him, he smiled. She would need encouragement. Not even he could let a woman feel as vulnerable as he was making her without at least giving her a pat on the head.

"Want to check under the hood, too?" Ah, there was that snark, that little defiant streak she couldn't quite tamp down.

"That's a good idea. Turn back around, bend over the bed, and pull your ass cheeks apart for me. I want to see everything. If I'm taking you on, taking you under my protection, everything you have, everything you are, belongs to me."

She swallowed. A slight movement of her throat, but one he caught. The gulp of a submissive who just heard the words that melted her insides, but that wasn't enough. He didn't want to just word-fuck her, he wanted to have every inch of her.

"You aren't moving, Addison." He kept his words firm. This was a teaching moment; start as you mean to go on, he'd been taught. "If you need help obeying, I'll help you, but it will cost you. Every time I have to make you, force you to obey, you'll be punished. So, understand that now before you make your next decision. I don't want what isn't freely given. You will give me your submission, you will give me your obedience."

Her breath came in shorter bursts, her breasts, those beautifully round pert tits, rose and fell with her breathing. Her arousal filled the room; he'd never smelled anything so potent, so delicate before.

She must not have wanted to tempt fate, because she turned back around to face the bed, bending over at the waist and pressing her face into the mattress. Her hands slipped behind her, grabbing her ass cheeks but then stilling. She groaned. He doubted it was meant for his ears, but he'd heard it. He felt the agony of her decision, of her giving over to him, and it turned him on even more. If that made him a bastard, that was fine with him.

"Addison, last warning." He wouldn't take much pleasure in making her. Taking her submission, taking what was given always gave sweeter vibes than making the girl. But every now and then he'd come across a sub who wanted him to make her. Those subs never lasted very long with him. He'd give them what they wanted, but there'd be a price and they rarely wanted to deal with that a second time. Maybe that was why he was still single, still looking for someone to be his full time. Or it was because he had more shit in his baggage than any one woman wanted to help him carry.

He sighed, ready to intervene, but she got herself going again. Her fingers gripped the insides of her cheeks and with gentle care pulled them apart, revealing her pussy, glistening with her desire, and the dark pucker of her asshole. Closing the gap between them, he lowered himself down on his haunches, getting face to ass with her.

"Fuck." He inhaled. "The scent of your pussy is filling up the room," he laughed. "No, don't let go. I didn't say that was a bad thing." He tapped her right hand when it started to lose its grip.

She groaned, and went back into position.

"So wet already, Addison. I've threatened to punish you. I've promised to make you give all of yourself to me, and you are near dripping." With his middle finger, he slid through her folds, down to her clit and circled the swollen nub. At his touch, her back arched, her ass propped up higher, and she moaned. Not the embarrassed sound of earlier when she was caught playing with herself. But a hopeful, full of desire melody that spoke to him on darker levels than he'd tapped into in a long time.

"Please, Trevor." A soft plea as she pressed back against his finger. He flicked the nub, laughing when she yelped.

"What, Addison? Remember, you have to ask, beg or I won't." He'd told her earlier he wouldn't give her release until she begged for it, and he was a man of his word.

She looked over her shoulder at him, her wide eyes finding his. "Trevor, please."

"Pull your cheeks further apart," was his response. She readjusted her position and did as he asked. "Have you been fucked here?" He tapped her little pucker with his thumb while his middle finger continued to dance over her clit.

"No." She shook her head. "Please." She arched more, pushing back.

"You understand this will make you mine, this will mean until we part ways, you'll do what I say, when I say, how I say, and if you don't, I will punish you." Two of his fingers were poised at her entrance.

"Yes, yes." She nodded, but it wasn't the consent of a logical thinking woman. He pulled his hand free and stood up. "Trevor!" She stomped her foot on the floor.

"Oh, acting the spoiled brat already?" He laughed and gave her two sharp slaps to her thighs with the flat of his hand.

"Ow!" She let go of her ass and started to stand up, but he pushed her back down.

"No, you stay down there. I'm getting a condom. Tell me now if you want this all to stop."

She licked her lips, biting at her lower corner.

"I don't want you to stop."

He picked up his pants that he'd left on the floor before getting into bed hours ago, and dug out a condom from his wallet. Once he'd shucked his boxers and rolled the latex over his throbbing cock, he looked back down at her. She'd watched every move he made.

"What do you want, Addison?" He stepped behind her again, lining up his cock with her pussy. He could feel the heat already coming off of her, the wetness of her passage seeping out onto the tip of his dick as he pressed it against her.

"I want you to fuck me, Trevor. God, please fuck me."

"Since you've been good. Keep those cheeks pulled apart for me and take your fucking." He gripped her hips and with one swift thrust he was inside of her, buried up to the hilt. She cried out as her tight pussy adjusted to being filled by him, and he stilled. Giving her a moment, as well as trying to regain control over his own cock. "Don't let go of those ass cheeks," he ordered through gritted teeth as he pulled back out and thrust forward again. The bed squeaked from the force of it.

"Fuck!" she cried out, starting to move in rhythm with him.

He grunted as he continued to fuck her, harder thrusts to match hers. She didn't just take her fucking, she was giving one back in return. His jaw hurt from being clenched, he couldn't wait much longer. The heated walls of her pussy were grabbing at him, trying to drain him of his release.

He reached around her, brushing over the patch of hair and found her clit. "So fucking ready for me." He rubbed his finger over the swollen bundle of nerves, faster.

"Oh! Oh!" To her credit, she didn't let go of her ass, she dug her nails into her own flesh to keep from disobeying him. That sight sent him over the edge.

"Come for me, Addison!" he demanded and pinched her clit. She began to howl, to buck back at him as though in a fevered frenzy. Her pussy clamped down on him, pulling every bit of release from him as he grunted back at her. His orgasm blinding him, he gripped her hips harder and thrust forward once, twice, and then he stilled, letting the waves of heaven capture the moment.

When he finally caught his breath, he slipped free of her, running his hand over her back, down to her ass and brushing her hands away. He sat beside her as he took care of the condom, tossing it in the trash can.

She hadn't moved from her position over the bed. Her shoulders shook, but there was no sound. Not being completely ignorant of women, he pulled her up and into his lap, scooting them back against the headboard.

He cradled her, letting her head rest against his shoulder as she cried. Silent tears ran off her cheek onto his shoulder, but he didn't push her, didn't ask anything of her, he just held her.

"I'm sorry," she said, sniffling and wiping the back of her wrist across her wet cheeks.

"It's been a rough day," he said and tightened his embrace.

She gave a short laugh. "It's been a rough year."

"You haven't been with anyone since your fiancé, have you?" The revelation struck him hard.

"I tried going to the club a few times, but it wasn't the same so I backed off. So, no. I haven't gone to bed with anyone."

He held her tighter, drawing her back to his chest and resting his chin on her head. He was a bastard. Knowing he'd been the first after such a long time made him want her again.

"Rest up, sweet-cheeks."

ADDISON WOKE to singing coming from the bathroom. Trevor was singing, a perfect tenor, too. She couldn't help but smile. It just seemed easy. Waking up in bed and hearing him in the next room. So much had changed in the last twenty-four hours she could barely get her mind around it.

She remembered the conversation they'd had before he'd touched her. Hell, he'd barely touched her, yet every fiber of her body had felt him. It was the strangest thing, to feel held by someone with just their words.

Had she really agreed to be his submissive? He

probably just meant it as foreplay. Excellent foreplay, but just words. She couldn't and wouldn't hold him to it. Besides they just met, and he was tasked with dragging her home. He said he wouldn't, and she had to trust him on that. She didn't really have a choice. If she didn't trust him, he couldn't help.

He'd held her as she cried, and when she'd finished, even after she'd cried all over him, he hadn't mocked her, or acted unaffected. He'd tucked her into bed, snuggled up next to her, and promised everything would look different in the morning. He promised the guilt would fade, that she wasn't a freak, she wasn't a 'two-dollar whore.' He had tensed when she voiced that concern, not knowing its origination, and only grew more irritated when she confessed it had been her father's favorite phrase to use against her. Especially when her father had found out about her visits to Leather and Lace.

Deciding she'd start the day out on the right foot, she jumped out of bed, only pausing a moment from the dull throb between her legs and searching out her clothes. Once dressed, she peeked out the window to find a donut shop across the street.

Trevor was still singing in the shower, and she didn't want to disturb him. She grabbed her purse and slipped out of the room, heading to the donut shop. A cup of coffee and some pastries would do them both good. Then they could plan out the day, or week, or however long he thought it would take to unravel the mess she was in.

Her stomach decided she should buy a full dozen donuts to go along with their coffees. She paid the cashier and scooped up the box, while balancing the cups of hot joe in her hands.

The smile on the cashier's face faded. She felt him. Could sense the anger rolling off of him before she even turned around. The look on the young woman's face told her everything. He was pissed.

Throwing on a radiant smile, she turned to face him. "Oh, Trevor." She tried to sound surprised, but she was sure he picked up on the little tremor. "I was just getting us breakfast, but since you're here, you can carry the coffee." She handed him the two hot cups, hoping that his silence would at least last until they were outside. His dark expression soured further when she brushed past him through the doors out into the parking lot.

"What the fuck were you doing, leaving the room without telling me?" he demanded once they were in the parking lot.

"We can talk when we get back to the room." She continued to uphold her pleasant tone, though she doubted if her plan was as solid as she thought.

"Oh, we are going to talk all right. Then we are going to strip, and then we are going to get spanked and then we are going to cry, and by we, I mean you."

After imparting that bit of knowledge on her, he stalked ahead of her, gripping the coffee cups so tight she worried he'd spill them.

He'd cool off once they were in the room and she explained. She'd only gone for coffee, it's not like she'd gotten in his car and taken off. He'd calm down, and they'd talk. Reasonably.

The motel door was open when she caught up to him; he was holding it open with his foot, the coffees taking up both of his hands while he glared at her. She was losing hope pretty quick that his temper was cooling. His jaw ticked beneath the tightness of it, his eyes were basically black, and even his hair looked angry standing up on end.

"Trevor, I was just getting breakfast, calm down." She placed the box of donuts on the table and wiped her hands on her jeans. He didn't look calm, or anywhere near it.

"Did I not make it clear last night?" He put the coffees on the dresser and stepped to her, only stopping once he was directly in front of her. He towered at least half a foot over her, making her crane her neck in order to look up at him. But given how tense his expression was at the moment, she found it more settling to stare at his chest. "Didn't I?" He sounded like he wanted to shake her.

"Yes. You said I had to listen to you. I get that, but

you didn't say I couldn't go get donuts." A valid point as far as she was concerned.

"Why didn't you tell me where you were going?"

"You were in the shower." This was going fine, next question.

"You couldn't open the door and tell me?" Point to him.

"Wasn't it locked?" She needed to firm up her voice if she was going to get out of the conversation unscathed.

"Do you think I would have said yes or no to you going alone across the street?"

She blinked. The answer to that question was going to seal her fate. She wasn't new to this dance, but she'd never quite learned how to perfect it. "How would I know?"

"Lying makes it worse. Answer me now, Addison." The same voice that had made her melt for him, crave him, and want everything he had to offer, now struck at her.

"No. You would have said no." She took a deep breath.

"So, you knew you shouldn't, and yet you did."

It occurred to her that she could sidestep him and get away, but she also remembered how lightning fast he could be, and she wasn't in the mood to be pinned to the bed again.

"Trevor." She sucked in a breath. "I'm sorry if you

were worried when you came out of the shower, but I was just getting donuts. I'll be more careful from now on. Okay?"

He eyed her quietly while her nerves danced. Either he'd pardon her or he'd execute, but it wasn't her call at the moment.

"What did you ask me last night before I fell asleep? The first time, before I found you with your fingers all over your pussy."

Her cheeks heated. The pulse in her neck beat hard. Why did he have to bring that up, either of those things? Why couldn't he be like most men and forget half of conversations?

"Trevor."

"My patience is pretty nonexistent at the moment, Addison." The warning would not go unheeded.

"I asked you if you'd spank me." Words hurt, she knew that, but it was usually when hearing them, not saying them.

"Now ask me again, ask me what you asked me last night." He took another step toward her, nearly eliminating any space between them.

She was going to regret it. "Will you spank me if I'm naughty?" The question came out in a clear whisper. If he wanted her to say it louder, he'd have to drag it out of her. Her throat was closing, her heart pounded, she wouldn't be able to give him anything more than that.

"Yes, Addison. Of course I will. And do you think you were naughty? Leaving without telling me? While you have crazy men after you, you walked out of here without protection or letting me know where you'd be. And I was in the shower, so if those assholes had been out in the parking lot, waiting for that door to open, and they'd been able to get in here when you opened it, how the fuck was I going to know or be prepared to help you? Run out here with my dick swinging in the wind?"

Under normal circumstances she'd find the image amusing, however, his lips were thin when he talked, and his eyes narrowed as he continued.

"So, were you naughty?"

She swallowed hard, tears already building in her eyes. "Yes."

"Take off your jeans and your panties, go stand in that corner with your hands on your head. I need a fucking minute." He pointed to the corner on the other side of the room, away from the window.

"Trevor—"

"Learn this now, Addison. When I say you're getting punished, you're getting punished. Any smart remarks, pleas for leniency, or attempts to dissuade me will only add to what you have coming. You got me?"

She nodded and raised her chin as she stepped around him to get in the corner he pointed to. Once there, she unbuttoned her jeans and shoved them down with her panties.

"All the way off, Addison," his rough voice dictated from behind her and she maneuvered her clothing down to her ankles and stepped out of them.

"Hands," he barked when she still hadn't put them on her head. "Stay there just like that."

The box of donuts opened, and she heard him rifling through. Really? He was going to eat one of the fucking donuts while he calmed down enough to spank her? A part of her wanted to turn around and flip him off, but the unease in her ass begged her to stay.

She rested her head on the wall after several minutes ticked by. Trevor wasn't the first dominant man she'd come across in the past year since losing Steven, but he was the first one she didn't want to run from. If that meant anything, she wasn't going to analyze it yet. First, she had to get through whatever he had planned, then she could figure it all out. Including how the hell she was going to get out of the mess she found herself in.

"Come here, Addison." A much calmer voice called out to her. She left her hands where they were and walked over to him. He sat on the edge of the bed, watching her as she moved to him. "Kneel." He pointed to the floor in front of him. She managed to move into position without taking her hands down, hoping that would count toward good behavior and get her out of some of the trouble she seemed to be in.

"I'm sorry, Trevor." Start off with an apology.

"You're sorry you're in trouble, not that you did what you did. You don't really think you did anything wrong." He shook his head. Steven had always taken her apology.

She didn't know what to say to that.

"I'm going to make you understand that I mean what I say. Any disobedience will be dealt with, and not easily. I'm not casual. I don't take this lightly."

"Trevor," she sighed. She'd just gone for fucking donuts!

"You knew I'd say no. You knew there are crazy assholes out searching for you, and you just decided to go off and get donuts. You knew all of this and did it anyway. You had no regard for your own safety or my authority. Your ass is mine until this is all over with, and that means when you act out, you get your ass blistered." He leaned back, unbuckling his belt and slowly pulling it from the loops.

She watched as the thick black leather was freed from his jeans and was looped in his hand.

"Now. Get up, and get over my lap. You can hold the bed, or my leg, you can cry and scream if you want, but you are not to kick or try to get up until I'm done. And when I'm done, you'll go right back in that corner until I say."

Addison moved back to her feet, noticing he had no intention to help her, and shifted to his right side. Steven had always pulled her over his lap. It was easier that way. This offering herself to him, it was worse. Way worse.

"I'm not interested in taking what isn't offered. Lie over my lap and accept your spanking." He watched her closely. The tension had eased in his jaw, and he was in complete control. Even if her own emotions were in turmoil trying to find a safe place to hide, he was all confidence.

She lowered her arms and managed to get over his lap without making too much of a fool of herself. Had she really signed up for this?

"Trevor. Wait." She didn't rise, but he didn't make any move to begin either. "You don't have to do this. I mean, I know what we said last night. But I'm not going to hold you to it, I mean, we don't even really know each other. So we had sex, no big deal. You aren't responsible for me. I mean I'm not yours, not really, so we don't have to do this."

When he didn't speak, she thought he was considering it, but when his hand made contact with her bare ass she knew otherwise.

"We'll talk about last night later. Right now, we are addressing this morning." Another hard swat to the other cheek. She wiggled, but did her best to stay put.

His hands had looked harmless enough, but now

that they were being applied to her ass, she was sure they were made of steel and not mere mortal bone. After a few dozen swats she clenched his leg, gulping in deep breaths. The burn was becoming unbearable, and staying still wasn't as easy as in the beginning.

His attention moved, focusing the swats to the back of her thighs.

She howled with the fresh burn and bucked up, but he'd been ready for her. Shifting his arm around her waist, he managed to keep her torso in place while continuing to lay into her ass unencumbered.

"Disobedience isn't tolerated, Addison," he said just after delivering a heated blow to her thigh.

"I know!" She squeezed his jeans into her fist and tried to find some corner in her mind to hide from the ferocious sting he continued to apply to her backside.

"There," he said after another swat, and she rested her head against the bed. That wasn't too bad, all things considered. Her ass was hot and a bit sore, but she'd live.

She should have known he wasn't done.

The first strike of the belt against her ass had her screaming out from the line of fire. The second and third blow landed one right on top of the other, both over her sit spots. She cried out again, but he had turned deaf to her pleas.

She scrambled on his lap, trying to move away

from the punishing leather. He held very little back, leaving no doubt to the seriousness of the discipline.

"Do you see what happens when you disobey?" The belt flicked across the up-curve of her ass. Even with the less intense swat, the sting turned up the heat of her ass. The man obviously knew how to deliver a blistering without giving too much.

"Yes! Yes!" she cried, feeling the tears running in hot streaks down her face. "Please."

"If you think I'll say no, do you think you should just go do it anyway?"

"No! No!" She shook her head to emphasize her answer, but another hot blow took her breath away. She'd never sit again, she was sure of it.

"Who owns this ass?" He patted her cheeks with his bare hand. "Who, Addison?" He slapped harder when she didn't answer.

She was gulping in air, sobbing from the burn in her ass, and he wanted to have a conversation.

"You do," she finally managed to croak out.

"That's right." The belt came down again and again. She kicked her feet and wiggled but it got her nothing. She made no strides in getting free or avoiding his punishment.

"I'm sorry! I'm sorry!" she cried out when he paused for a moment. "I'll listen. I'll be good. I swear!" she begged as the tears dripped down her face.

He'd already stopped spanking her.

"Shhh... it's okay. It's okay." One hand rubbed her back, while the other rested on the burning embers of her ass. Her body slacked over his lap. Her breath caught up to the rest of her, and her heart calmed to a steady beat. But the pulsing in her ass hadn't subsided, and she doubted it would for some time to come.

"When you're ready, back in the corner." The scolding disappeared from his tone.

She sniffled and nodded, pushing herself up. He let her off his lap, but clasped her hands in front of her.

"Five minutes," he said, wiping away the dampness of her cheeks. He stood from the bed, capturing her face in his hands and bringing his mouth down on hers.

His kiss deepened when she put her hands on his hips. Her core, already awake from the discipline, reacted to his touch with a fierceness that overrode the burning throb in her backside. Her hands went up to his shoulders, finding solace in the strength of his body, and comfort in the warmth of his kiss.

When he broke off the kiss, he looked at the corner. "Five minutes." He turned her around, sending her on her way with a swat to her ass.

She wandered over to the corner, not looking back at him, not giving any backtalk. She couldn't. Her lips tingled too brightly from his kiss for her to do anything other than exactly what he'd instructed.

8

Dragging his belt back through the loops in his jeans, Trevor kept an eye on the woman in the corner. She had her forehead pressed against the wall, and her shoulders gently shook. Her distress could have come from the embarrassment of the punishment, or the pain of the spanking, or it could very well be the height of her arousal.

With all the kicking she'd done he had been able to catch a glimpse of her glistening pussy lips, and when she had stood to her full height the sweet smell of her juices wafted upward. The physical and emotional reactions didn't match up for her, and he'd seen enough submissives get horny after a punishment to know the difference. Either feeling sorry for herself or genuinely feeling remorseful did not change the raging urge to get fucked that her body portrayed.

Not that she didn't want and deserve a good hard fucking. And the devil knew Trevor was up for the task, but not after a punishment. At least not this time. She needed to learn: bad girls face bad consequences.

A shiver ran down her back when his belt buckle jingled as he finished buckling himself up. A submissive's body language couldn't be ignored. Too fucking pretty.

"Are you sorry for yourself or for what you did?" he asked, stepping behind her.

She shook her head.

"Use your words. I don't like nonverbal answers."

She heaved a heavy sigh, exasperation most likely. "I'm fine." The sniffle betrayed her.

"That wasn't an answer to my question. Try again." He ran his fingers up her arm, feeling the tension in her muscles and wishing he hadn't just whipped her. She needed a release.

"Both. I'm sorry for both." Pressing her body further into the corner, she avoided looking at him.

Splaying his hand over her back, he rubbed. "Well, being sorry for what you did is good; it means you might actually think before you do it again. Feeling sorry for yourself is a big waste of time." Moving down her to her ass, he cupped her still warm and red ass cheek. "You've been punished and forgiven. It's over." Breaking his own fucking rule, he slid his hand lower, following the curve of her ass until his fingers felt the warmth of her pussy. "Except for this." He rimmed her entrance, holding back a laugh when she opened her legs enough for him to have free range of her body. "This part will last a few more hours. No way you're getting an orgasm right now. Maybe later, but not right now. So, this wet, hot pussy is going to suffer. For that, I am sorry, but it can't be helped." He thrust two fingers into her passage, letting her arch back at him, nearly wagging her ass at him. He pumped hard into her half a dozen times then pulled out.

"Bastard," she pouted and stood back at her full height.

He licked his two fingers, making sure to slurp and pop his fingers out of his mouth for her. "No, I had a father. Complete asshole, but still, a father." He patted her ass again and pressed his body against her back, pushing her against the wall. "Your time's up. Now be a good girl, take a quick shower, and we can eat those donuts you got us."

With two hands pressed against the wall she pushed away, almost knocking him over. He'd give her a solid A for effort.

"And I'm sure you know touching yourself right now would be a bad idea."

She flipped him off as she walked into the bathroom, right before she slammed the door. He let himself enjoy a soft laugh. He should drag her out of there and teach her another lesson about respect, but he found her too damn cute at the moment. The woman had walked away from him with a glowing red ass and still had the gumption to flip him off? Some fires weren't meant to be put out, only controlled.

After several minutes passed and he didn't hear much movement in the bathroom, he decided to check on her. Not that it would benefit her in the least, but there was a window in there she could have shimmied out of. Running away bare-assed would be completely stupid, but she'd been a bit pissed when she walked away.

To his surprise the door was unlocked. Easing the door open, he peeked in. The solid beige shower curtain was drawn, keeping her out of his view. Shaking his head at his own dirty thoughts, he started to close the door, and that's when he heard it.

"Oh, god." The soft whisper of a woman close to release. "Oh, fuck." The shower curtain moved, bunched up as though she were clutching it from inside the shower. It was only held by a cheap plastic rail; she'd yank the damn thing down pretty soon.

He leaned against the wall, one ankle hooked over the other and his arms crossed. He could stop her, should stop her, but she'd already dug the hole, why not let herself get buried in it too.

Her heavy breaths started to come in shorter bursts, faster and faster. He imagined her inside the shower, one hand holding the curtain, while the other saw to her carnal needs. Was she playing with just her clit or was she fingering herself? She'd needed her clit played with the night before. The memory of that coupling combined with her soft moans got his cock's full attention. Not that it wasn't already at full mast from having her ass bouncing beneath his hand only minutes ago. Shit. He'd just fucking punished her, and there she was disobeying him. Again.

Hard dick or not, things needed settling and the sooner the better for them both.

"If you come, you'll be getting more than a spanking when you get out here." He said the words just as she barreled over her edge. She sucked in a shocked breath, but the curtain shook, she cursed, and her breath was just as raspy as before. She'd come, and he'd most likely ruined it for her.

He smiled. Good.

"Trevor." The curtain righted itself and the water turned off. "I was just taking a shower." She lied pretty well when she wasn't looking right at him. He'd have to see how she did when his face was right up against hers.

"Dry off and get out here, then you can try that again." He yanked the curtain back, taking as much time as he liked to look her over. Water droplets ran down her chest, over the hardened peaks of her nipples, down her tummy, over her rounded hips, and down her thick thighs. Feeling the strain in his pants, he shoved a towel at her. "Dry off."

She took the towel, shaking out the folds and went about doing what she was told. Not sure his cock could handle any more, he growled and walked out of the bathroom and waited for her in the bedroom.

She'd come. She'd come and he hadn't. That wasn't a big deal, really. Plenty of times he'd brought his subs to orgasm and left himself wanting. But that was when they'd deserved it, when he was pleasuring and rewarding. Addison hadn't earned a reward. She'd earned a punishment, which she'd taken pretty well. It was her own damn fault that it turned her on, that was part of it. No rewards, no fucking orgasms after getting your ass blistered for being bad.

By the time, she stepped out of the bathroom, he had his lust mostly in hand. Her hair lay limp and soaked around her shoulders, while the rest of her was wrapped up in the towel. Her hands clutched at the top of the towel, her throat working hard when she swallowed.

"Did your boyfriend ever punish you?" He needed to know what he was dealing with.

"Steven? Yeah. You saw, remember?" A fresh blush took over her cheeks at the snappy comment. In an attempt to annoy him, she'd embarrassed herself.

"I also remember you coming unglued shortly after. He fucked you right there, didn't he?" He'd heard, rather than saw, that part of their scene. Addison wasn't quiet when it came to her release.

"Yeah, so?" The defiance was back in full force.

"So, did you really try to stay out of trouble? I mean, I'm sure you didn't like getting into trouble, but was there ever a time you pushed him to get a punishment, because the sex afterwards was worth it?"

"What? No! Why would I do that? I could just ask for spanking, or a scene."

"Yeah, but a punishment scene is different." He rounded her, walking around her as he spoke. Tiny goose pimples lined her arms. He hadn't turned on the heat in the room.

She took a deep breath. "I really don't want to talk about this. All of this is just stupid." She tried to walk past him toward the bed where she'd already laid out her bag. He grabbed her arm and spun her around.

"Answer me."

She looked up at the ceiling. "Fine."

"What?" He gave her a little shake.

"Fine. I probably did."

He let her go, and stood in front of her. "I don't like games, Addison. So, I don't ever let my subs come after they've been punished. That way, there's no games like that."

"I'm not really your sub," she stated flatly.

He tilted his head and smiled. "Until I have you safely out of this shit storm you find yourself in, you are. Unless you'd like me to just take you back to Daddy?"

Her eyes narrowed, her lips pressed together in a thin line. "You really are a bastard."

"I already told you. I have a father." Had. Have. The man was alive somewhere, but he never earned the right to be called Dad. Not after the shit he put his mother and Devin through. "So, do you agree, or are you going to keep fighting me?"

Her nostrils flared just a bit, enough for him to know he'd gotten to her. A little more coercion than he otherwise would feel comfortable with, but ever since he'd laid eyes on the woman, his darker side begged to be played with.

"Yes, I agree."

He clapped his hands and rubbed them together. "Excellent." Ripping the towel from her body, he pointed to the bed. "Bend over."

"But—"

"Yes, Addison. I want your butt in the air. Oh, don't worry, you're not getting another spanking. I don't intend to leave bruises, but you aren't getting away with stealing my orgasm. Now, over." He grabbed her elbow and all but flung her at the bed.

Once she was in position, her arms flat on the bed, her ass high in the air, she looked over her shoulder. If there had been fear, he would have stopped. It would have killed him, but he would have. But she looked at him with nothing resembling that. Wide eyes filled with curiosity as he moved behind her.

"Your orgasms, just like the rest of you, belong to me. If you steal one, there's a price. I bet right now, you'd love to have my cock in you. Filling you, stretching you. That piddly little orgasm you had wouldn't come close to what I could give you in this position." The tips of his fingers trailed over the still red stripes from his belt.

Her cheeks clenched when he unbuckled his belt for the second time that morning. He hadn't lied, he wasn't going to spank her again. Another need would be filled this time.

"I bet your cunt is still soaked, still wanting." He pulled his cock out of his pants, fisting it, and began to pump his staff. "I bet you'd fucking love to have my cock again."

WHATEVER HE WAS DOING behind her, it wasn't at all what she wanted. Which was probably the point. Finally, she looked at him again, and her eyes were immediately drawn to his cock. Catching her looking, a smirk crossed his lips. He unhanded himself and bent over, offering his palm to her.

"Spit," he ordered. Not wanting to, but seeing the look in his eyes, she decided it might be best to start playing by his rules. Her ass already burned, her pussy felt empty, and he'd ruined her orgasm in the shower with his well-timed announcement.

She gathered up as much saliva as she could and emptied it onto his palm.

"Good girl." He winked at her and brought his hand back to his dick, wrapping it around once more and stroking himself. Those two words would be better said before he slid his cock into her, not when he was denying her the very thing she wanted. "Keep your eyes on me," he ordered when she resolved not to watch him.

Long strokes of his hand left her jealous. If he wanted an orgasm, she'd be happy to help. All he had to do was stop teasing her. She candidly licked her lips, wondering how full her mouth would be with his thick cock inside of it. She imagined him choking her with it, not caring, and still fucking her face. Her body reacted to the images as though the act were taking place. She had to get him inside of her.

He leaned over her, one hand on the bed beside her while the other worked harder on his cock. "Fuck," he grunted. Every now and then the head of his cock would brush her sore ass, but other than that he did not touch her. "I can smell your cunt, it's so wet. You want me."

"Please?" She heard herself beg before she realized it was going to happen.

He laughed. "Shit, your ass is so hot, so damn hot." The hand on the bed moved to her shoulder, holding her in place as he jerked his cock even more. "Fuck." Hot ribbons of cum streamed out of him and onto her ass and back. Each milky white spurt landed with a grunt from him. When he finally spent everything, he released her shoulder and moved back. She heard the zipper, the buckle and thought it was over. "No, stay down."

"Can you get me a rag?" she asked, trying not to sound disappointed that he hadn't fucked her.

He laughed again. "Nope. Not yet."

She looked over her shoulder again, finding his thumb in his mouth. It made a loud pop when he pulled it free of his lips. Unsure of what he was doing, she yelped when his hands spread her ass cheeks wide. Wider than was comfortable, though she doubted he cared about her comfort at that moment.

The wet pad of his thumb circled the tight pucker of her ass. She tried to clench, to tighten, but he only pinched her ass hard. "No. Stay. This is part of your punishment."

Her resistance was a waste. His thumb squirmed right into her backside. The pressure and embarrassment was too much, and she rested her head on the mattress. "No. Please. No."

He stilled. "Addison, if you really mean no, say Master."

Her face was once again ablaze. Now he was giving her a safeword? With his thumb up her ass? It was too much, all of it too much. And the worst part, her pussy was clenching down, looking for relief. He was only making her more aroused, not less with the humiliation of his cum slipping down her back, and his thumb where she'd never let anyone or anything go before.

"Last chance."

She realized he was giving her time to say the word, to call off the embarrassing act.

She took a deep breath and clenched her eyes closed.

"That's a good girl." And when he said it, it wasn't sarcastic, or fake, or condescending. Pride laced those words. "I don't have my plugs with me, so you'll have to deal with my finger." He patted her rump with his free hand and thrust his thumb even further into her backside. She squirmed, but didn't try to get away from him.

"Now. With my thumb plugging your ass, my cum dripping all over your back and your ass, tell me what you did wrong, and what you'll do in the future."

Was he kidding? It wasn't enough that he'd humiliated her? Now he wanted to talk about it? When she felt another pinch to her ass she yelped and decided to get to it.

"I had an orgasm when you told me not to." His

thumb retracted only to push in again and she growled. "And in the future, I won't disobey your rules." Saying that sentence, those words, brought about a calm to her chest she hadn't felt in a very long time. His rules. Obeying his rules. Her breath steadied, and she opened her eyes, expecting to see him gloating.

But instead, all she found was respect.

"Good." He pulled his thumb out and stood at full height. "Go wash up again. In the future, I won't be nice and let you wash, you'll just sit with my cum all over your back." He walked into the bathroom, leaving her bent over the bed.

9

H e was losing his mind. That's the only reasonable explanation to explain why he was taking them down their current path.

Trevor watched the road with more intensity than he probably needed, as he put miles between them and the motel. It had been quiet in the car since they pulled out of the parking lot and hit the highway, and he was grateful for the peace.

Except all the quiet kept leading him back to the same place in his mind. He'd lost all sense.

Cowsky had given him the go-ahead to take as much time as he needed, putting him on official vacation during their conversation earlier. Trevor hadn't told him about the evidence she held over her father and the Stephanos family. Even with the amount of trust he had in his commander, it wouldn't be safe to give that information to anyone at the precinct. If her father came demanding information, Cowsky needed to be able to say he had none.

Taking on this situation, putting himself between Addison and an organized crime family, was crazy. And completely his brother's fault. If he hadn't grown up watching Devin constantly doing the right thing, and always looking out for those who couldn't protect themselves, he wouldn't have had the same damn trait embedded in him.

God damn hero complex is what it was.

But it was one thing to decide to help her when obviously she needed help, but to make her his sub? To fuck her, punish her, and then the thing with her ass? His jaw started to throb from the tension, but it was his own fault.

"So, exactly where are we going?" Addison broke the silence in the car after an hour and a half of driving.

After she'd washed the second time, he'd thrown some clothes at her and told her to dress. She hadn't looked happy with what he had pulled out of her bag for her, but she hadn't complained either.

"I don't know," he admitted. They couldn't go back to the city. Not with her father and the Stephanos brothers looking for her. They needed somewhere to hide out for a little while until he was able to get some real help from the precinct.

He'd already tried his brother, but he had his own fucking mess to deal with, and Blake, a good friend of his, wasn't answering his phone.

"So, we're just going to drive around aimlessly?" The snark was back in her tone but with less malice. After she'd given him her word she'd obey his rules, it was as though some huge weight had been pulled from her shoulders. He didn't dare think it had anything to do with him. No, it was the endorphins from their morning activities, that was all.

"No. I'm waiting for a call back. A friend has a cabin up this way, we used it for fishing a few times, but I don't have the current passcode for the box. By the time, we get there, we should be good."

"So, you do know where we're going," she pointed out.

He looked over at her. She'd braided her hair again and was starting to loosen it up with her fingers to take it out. "Why do you that?"

"Do what?" she asked, furrowing her brow.

"Your hair, you braid it then take it out right away. Why?" He had a pretty good idea, but wondered if she even realized it.

"Oh." She looked down at her fingers and laughed, confirming what he thought. "I'm not sure."

"You busy your hands when you're nervous. So, what has you anxious right now? Being alone with me?"

"No." She finished taking out the braid and tucked her hands beneath her legs, as though to keep them from repeating the action.

He didn't buy it, but he'd let her have her privacy for a little longer.

The orange hue in the sky deepened the longer they drove, making the scenery a bit more interesting to take in as they continued down the highway.

"So, what's with your father anyway? Why was he so hell bent on keeping you in Chicago?" If she wouldn't open up about whatever bothered her at the present moment, he could at least extract some information about her father.

She took a deep breath and looked out the window. "I used to think it was out of fear of being alone. My mother walked out on us when I was young, seven maybe. He always seemed like the best father, paid extra attention to my schoolwork, came to all my school events, talked with my teachers. When I was older I recognized it for what it was, control. But I just thought he was afraid I'd leave him, too. Like my mom."

Trevor gripped the wheel a little tighter. He couldn't imagine what his life would have been like without his mother's unwavering support and love. His father hadn't been around, and thankfully so, but he'd at least had Devin. Although not the same, he'd still had two people in his life he could count on for safety and unconditional love.

"Your mom never tried to contact you?" he asked, busying his eyes with the task of checking the mirrors.

"No. I tried to track her down once though when I was fifteen." Her hands, he noticed, were working on her braid again, but he didn't mention it. "I was able to find a friend of hers, but she didn't know where my mom was. All she would tell me is my father hadn't made it easy for her when she was with us. She said he was controlling and cruel." She laughed. "She even asked me if I felt safe going home that night."

"Did you? Feel safe at home?"

"My father never struck me. He was just over-bearing and controlling. And when I started doing things for myself and stopped trying to get his approval, he lashed out, but I wasn't afraid of him. He could take away my trust fund or my car; those things never mattered to me anyway."

She finished unbraiding her hair and looked at her hands.

"I know I make it sound like he was a cruel man, but he was just—well, him. My mother walking out hurt him. Keeping me nearby meant he could still control me, or at least try. He was protecting himself from getting hurt again, I guess."

When he glanced over at her he thought he'd find sadness in her expression, but all he saw was resolve.

She had learned at a young age to depend only on herself. Because Daddy could take everything away and use it as a carrot to get what he wanted, and Mommy hadn't stuck around to protect her from the bastard.

"Fathers are supposed to protect their daughters, encourage them, and challenge them, not lock them up in little boxes and control their lives." They were also supposed to not raise their hands to their wives or their kids, but as his own father proved, not all fathers were up to the task of doing their jobs.

"And mothers aren't supposed to abandon their children." She gave a weak smile. "I think you know that, though."

"I won't lie, my mom was the best." He couldn't help but grin with that statement. His mother had gone through hell, but not once did the flames make their way back to his childhood.

"Which is probably why you're a detective searching out missing children, and I'm on the run from my father and his cronies." She forced a laugh, but it didn't reach her eyes.

The car fell into silence that stretched out between them. A comfortable quiet as the car rolled down the highway.

They were getting close to the turnoff when his phone finally started ringing.

"Blake," he answered. Finally.

"Got yourself in some trouble I see."

"Nope, no trouble. And nothing I can't handle. Just need that cabin for a day or two, until I get ducks lined up."

"And you can't go to the farmhouse because Devin has his own shit going on there. You know, between you two, I'm not sure I'll ever be paid back all the favors you owe me." He wasn't wrong. Blake got them out of more hot water over the years than either of them could ever hope to do for him. But it wasn't all their fault. Blake just had a knack for that sort of thing. Swooping in at the end to save everyone, it's just what he did.

"Yeah. So, can I use the damn cabin?" He didn't mean to sound testy, but Addison was watching him, trying to hear the conversation. She obviously never heard about what happened to the cat with all the curiosity.

Blake laughed. "Of course, dumbass. I'll text the code to you; it's a little longer than it used to be."

"Of course it is." Trevor laughed at his own bad joke.

"Amateur. You sure everything's good?"

Trevor glanced back over at Addison, braid half done. "It's going to be fine. I need one more favor. I have to get in touch with someone in the homicide department that's reliable. Someone not paid for. You know anyone?"

"A few, but not in your precinct."

"That's fine, I just need someone who can get records and maybe do a little digging."

"Okay. Text me what you're looking for, and I'll get it to them."

"Great. Thanks. Put it on my tab."

"Uh huh."

A minute later his phone buzzed with the code, and he turned off the highway toward the cabin.

"So, you aren't into master/slave stuff?" Addison surprised him with the change of topic.

When he glanced over at her, she was staring at the phone on the console buzzing again.

"Why do you say that?"

"The safeword you gave me. Master. You wouldn't give that to someone if you wanted them to call you that for real, or to think of you that way."

It had been a quick decision giving her that word. "I'm not into labels really. High protocol and all that, not really my thing. I'm simple. What I care about is respect and obedience."

If the dim lighting wasn't getting in his way, he noticed her shoulders drop a bit. "So, not dom/sub and all that?"

"Well, no, not really. I'm the dom and you're the sub, but that's about as far into roles I go."

"Oh." She looked out the window again. "The

sunset always looks so much more orange in the fall, it's pretty."

He wasn't letting her drive the conversation off course, not after she had chosen the subject. "You and Steven, you were master and slave?"

"No. I mean, he never collared me or anything. He was my sir, I guess you'd call it."

Trevor pulled the car down another road, feeling the paved road turn to gravel beneath the tires.

"You wanted him to collar you?"

She tensed beside him, pressing herself further against the door.

"It had to be hard. To lose him like that. I can't imagine having to bury someone I was engaged to." He wanted to kick his mouth's ass for spewing that out like that. The last thing she needed was another reason to close up on him.

"I didn't."

"Didn't what?" He leaned over the steering wheel watching for the last turn that would take them to the cabin. The sun was nearly gone at this point and it was getting harder to see even with the headlights.

"I didn't go to the funeral. His family lives out of state, up in Minnesota. That's where we were planning on moving. The police told me there wasn't much to identify, that the car had been on fire when they got on scene. His family had him cremated and they brought his ashes home. They had a memorial, but Daddy wouldn't let me go alone. Said he couldn't go with me and I was too emotional to do it alone. When he offered to let Jesse take me, I decided to stay home."

"Jesse Stephanos?"

"Yeah. The guy my father wants me to marry."

Trevor let out a low whistle. "He knows it's 2016, right?" Finally catching sight of the road, he cut the wheel.

She laughed. "Yeah. I tried explaining that. He thinks he can control everything, and when he can't, he plays dirty. I wanted to move out of the city. He said it wouldn't look good for his daughter to take a teaching position in one of the suburbs. Apparently, one of his friends is on the board of education, and he was trying to get more teachers into the public sector or something. I don't know, but I was quickly blackballed. The only position I could get was in CPS."

"So you're a teacher?"

"Not right now. I took a leave of absence after Steven died."

The car rocked and bounced from the rough road until he finally found the paved drive that took them the rest of the way. Blake could have had the whole damn road paved, but he only bothered with his drive-way. No one else lived up that high on the trail, so he didn't really care. His SUV could get up with no problem, but Trevor's little sedan didn't have as much balls.

"Here." He let out a long breath once they were on smooth pavement and driving up to the garage.

"I thought you said it was a cabin." She leaned toward the dash to get a better look.

"It's been in his family forever. There's only two floors, to them it's a cabin."

"It's fucking huge," she whispered.

"One, language. Two, surely you've seen bigger."

She giggled. Actually, giggled at his statement. "Well, I didn't want to offend."

"Oh, yeah? We'll see who's laughing after you cook us some dinner." He cut the engine and shot her a smile. "Blake was just up here last week, restocking the pantries and the freezer. Let's go see what we can find."

THE PANTRY WAS BIGGER than her closet back home. Not that she was a snob; she never cared about her father's money or anyone else's. Making her own way had always been her drive, but she had enjoyed her walk-in closet full of clothes.

Trevor went about checking all the room and the lights or something, while she fixed them dinner. She'd only half heard what he was saying, because he'd taken his shirt off while he'd said it. Why he needed his shirt off didn't make sense, but it probably would have had she been listening to him and not memorizing the sculpted body being laid out before her.

"What did you find?" He sauntered into the kitchen, with wet hair and fresh clothes on. Shower. That's what he'd done, he'd taken a shower.

"Spaghetti." She waved a hand over the pot of boiling water. "Didn't you shower this morning?"

"Yeah, and then I got all dirty when I went into the crawlspace to turn the water on." He'd mentioned something about that earlier, too.

"Oh." She turned away before he could see the blush on her cheeks. She really needed to get a handle on her cheeks. Blushing wasn't sexy, it was a sign of weakness. Did she want to be sexy for him? For Trevor?

"Everything's locked up and secured. Blake has a security system on the property so even if someone did have an idea of where we are, we'd know about it before they saw the lights in the house." He leaned one hip against the counter next to the stove and picked up a fork, dipping it into the noodles and pulling out one. She watched as he raised it over his mouth and nibbled on the steaming pasta. "Hmm. I'd take that off the heat now." He pointed toward the pot with the fork and put it back on the counter.

She put the strainer she'd found in the sink and grabbed the pot, forgetting that it was not her pot from home and the handle, like the pot, was made of stainless steel. She yelped and dropped the pot back onto the burner.

"Shit."

Trevor grabbed her hands and yanked her to the sink, turning on the cold water he thrust them under. "What the hell was that? What were you thinking?" he demanded.

"It was an accident, obviously," she yelled back at him. The burning cooled under the water, but she knew as soon as the water was gone the pain would simmer and settle.

"Potholders!" He jerked his chin to the two square potholders sitting next to the stove.

"I'm aware of what they are." She slammed her hips into him. "I'm fine. Just let go." She tried to yank her hands out of his grasp, but he only gripped her wrists harder.

"Let me see." He pulled her hands out of the water and inspected them. "Not as bad as I thought." He raised his eyes to hers. "You were distracted."

She huffed. Of course, she was distracted. The man was nothing but a distraction. "I'm fine," she said again, trying to pull her dripping hands from his grasp.

"Go upstairs to the bathroom. There's some aloe under the sink. I'll be up in a minute to wrap your hands. I'm gonna get the noodles off the stove."

"I can handle it. I'll be right back." She tried to turn, but he hadn't let go of her yet.

"When I get up there, I want you sitting on the counter, hands in your lap. If you so much as open a fucking cabinet door, you'll regret it."

She rolled her eyes. "Fine. Have it your way."

He yanked her back by her wrists when she tried to turn away again. He leaned down, completely invading her personal space. To her credit, she managed to keep herself planted and not step further back.

"That's right, sweet-cheeks. My way." If he was trying to intimidate her with his growly voice, it was working. He looked more dangerous when he was in protective mode. His eyes darkened more, his voice lowered, even his body seemed bigger.

"I already said okay."

His lips pulled up into a grin. "I would rather you said something else. What do you think I would rather you say?"

Her hands were starting to burn without the cold water running over her palms, but she ignored it. The heat simmering in the small space between them was hotter.

"Yes, Sir?" If he laughed, she'd kill him.

"Almost, try again without the question."

Her throat dried while she could feel perspiration

starting to form under her arms. If he was trying to make a point, consider it made.

"Yes, Sir." More confident this time. She expected a nod, a pat on the head maybe, but that's not what she got.

He let go of her wrists in exchange for grabbing her shoulders, drawing her up to him and capturing her mouth beneath his. One hand moved to the nape of her neck. It wasn't a sweet kiss, not even tender. Possessive. A man claiming what was his. She didn't try to escape it. Her heart fluttered beneath his power as his tongue swept into her mouth, his teeth nipping at her lips.

When he finally released her, he kept his hand at her neck as though to keep her positioned should he decide he wanted to taste her again. His pressed his nose against hers, his warm breath fanning her face. "That's more like it. Now go. Be a good girl for me." He gave her hair a little tug and completely untangled himself from her. A chill smacked her when he stepped away.

Forcing herself not to look stupid, she nodded and walked away, looking for the stairs. She wouldn't ask him, she'd find them and head to the bathroom. There had to be a mirror up there, so she could see if her lips really were bruised and swollen or if he'd just made them feel that way.

The cabin had a completely open floor plan, so it

wasn't hard to find the stairs or the bathroom. What was hard was trying to get up on the countertop without using her hands. She wouldn't categorize herself as short, but she wasn't tall enough to simply scoot up on the marble countertop, and using her hands was completely out of the question.

That's how he found her, trying to hop onto the countertop. She saw him out of the corner of her eye as her ass barely made contact with the edge and she slipped off again. Lucky for him, he didn't laugh. He only leaned against the door frame watching with piqued interest.

"Were you going to ask for help, or just keep trying until you broke your ass?"

She pinched her lips together to keep from saying something stupid and settled for giving him a pointed look. "I was trying to get up on the counter, but my fucking hands hurt too much. If you'd just let me take care of it myself I wouldn't need to get on the damn counter anyway." She had started out the right way, but quickly diverted into a gray area.

"One. Language, again. Last warning on that one, sweet-cheeks. Two. You being capable of fixing it yourself isn't the problem or point." He pushed off the door frame and sauntered into the bathroom. He waved a hand to move her from the cabinet and squatted down to gather his tools: white cotton wrappings and the aloe.

He placed everything on the counter and before she could step away or stop him, he hoisted her up by her waist, placing her next to the items.

"It's unnerving how you can do that without even a grunt," she muttered when he took her hands in his.

He laughed. "Grunt?"

"I'm not exactly tiny," she remarked, watching him squeeze the green goop onto her palm.

"Thank god for that." He winked and gently rubbed the sticky concoction into her skin. "Still hurt a lot?"

"No." She shook her head and continued to keep her eyes on him while he lubed up her second palm and then went about wrapping them both.

"You're lucky you didn't completely grab those handles. Your fingers would be hurting too," he commented, fully attentive to his task. When he was all done, he put everything away and placed his hands on the countertop, caging her in. "Now. About the cursing. No more. If you do it again, I'll soap your mouth."

He wasn't kidding, or if he was, he hid it really well.

"I'm an adult, Trevor," she sighed.

"Yeah, I know, but I hate it. Girls shouldn't curse."

"You're sexist. Huh, didn't see that one." She forced a laugh, trying to ease the tension rising between them. It was his fault; he was too close to her, and things got foggy when he stood so close.

"Let me rephrase my statement. *My* girl shouldn't curse."

His girl? At least for the time being, that's what he'd said. His little game for them to get through the time together until he could get her out of the mess she'd gotten herself into.

"Okay. No cursing. Got it. I think I can manage that for a few days. I should be able to go home in a few days, right?"

He ran a finger over her forehead, moving a piece of hair from her face. "I'm working on it. Hopefully, I'll know something tomorrow."

"Okay."

"Dinner's ready." He pushed off from the counter and helped her off the edge, giving her a quick slap to her ass. Which seemed to be his favorite way of getting her going.

10

———

Trevor didn't like what he was seeing. Blake had connected him with a guy from the homicide division who could be useful, except once Mark, the contact, heard the names Stephanos and St. Claire together he'd been less excited. Mark didn't back out of helping, but he made sure Trevor knew what sort of shit stew he was stirring up.

Within an hour, Mark had sent him over a few files, and none of it was helpful. Cover-ups, politicians paying each other off, all of it would make his job harder than it needed to be. Trevor knew it was a long shot. Even if he could prove her father had her fiancé killed, and that the Stephanos family was involved, that wouldn't exactly make Chicago safe for her. There wasn't just one Stephanos, it was a whole family, organized and connected. If she were responsible for taking down one of them, they'd come after her. If she did nothing, they'd come for her because she knew things she wasn't supposed to know.

Catch-22, welcome home.

He heard talking coming from the living room. Addison had still been asleep when he came down to make coffee. After they'd eaten dinner, he'd forced her to take a long bath in the Jacuzzi tub. She'd wanted to look over the files she had again, but he poured her some wine and sent her for a bath and then tucked her into bed. It had taken everything in him not to climb in after her, yank off her panties, and dive into her body. Which made it even harder in the morning, when he looked in on her and found her cuddling with a pillow, hair a tousled mess, and her mouth half open. If she'd been drooling on the pillow, it still wouldn't have made her any less beautiful. She just had that natural attractiveness, and no amount of dirt or grime would cover it up.

Sleeping in the other bedroom had been his decision, and he regretted it. He wouldn't do it again. He'd stayed up most of the night listening for her, checking on her, and walking the hallway. No, tonight he'd sleep right next to her.

He put his phone and coffee mug down and went into the living room.

In a pair of pajama bottoms and an oversized t-shirt she padded around the room in bare feet, chattering on the phone.

"I'm so sorry, Charity. I didn't tell you where I was going because I was afraid he'd show up at your apartment. I just didn't think he'd be so—fuck, I'm sorry." She hadn't noticed him yet, so she couldn't see the scowl forming on his face. Maybe she didn't understand the 'no cursing' rule wasn't just for around him. "Did he hurt you? What about Jackson, is he okay?" That didn't sound good at all.

Trevor watched her pace around the coffee table. The woman was walking in circles.

"Thank god. Okay, I'll call him. I'll take care of it. I promise. Did you tell him where I was?" There was a pause. "My phone? Wait, what?"

Trevor's ears perked up, and he all but leapt over the couch to get to her and yank the phone from her hand. He ended the call, and quickly went about destroying the phone, not stopping until it was in a handful of pieces.

Addison screamed at him the whole time, slapping at his arms when he kept the phone out of her reach. "What the hell are you doing? I was using that!"

Once it was unrepairable, he dropped the pieces to the couch. "Your phone. That's how your father found you the first time. I assumed it was your paychecks or something to do with work. Did you have your phone on at the apartment?"

She looked down at the tattered pieces of her phone and then glared at him. "You didn't need to break it," she shouted. "I could have just turned it off."

"No." He bent down and rummaged around until he found the little chip, holding it up for her. "This little thing here is a tracking device. Even with it off, it omits a signal. Your apartment was in such a rural area the signal may not have been strong enough for it to be picked up easily, but at work it gave your exact location."

She stared at the tiny chip in his hand. "My father had me chipped?"

"You're not really surprised, are you?" He dropped the chip back onto the pile. "And watch your mouth even if you think I can't hear you."

Her eyes narrowed, and her lips pinched together. "Seriously? That's what you want to say right now? That's the big concern? Because I cursed on the phone with my friend. My friend, who probably thinks I've been kidnapped because you didn't let me tell her goodbye."

"Who showed up at her place? Your dad or a Stephanos?"

Her eye widened with his question. "Jesse."

"And did she call you, or you call her?"

"She called me last night, after he'd stopped by. I saw the missed call this morning and called back." The pieces were coming together for her, and he watched as the fear and anger washed over her expressions. "Do you think they'll know where we are now?"

"I don't know. Probably not, since we're deep in the woods. Like I said, even if they do track us down, we'll know before they get close to the house."

At least that's what he kept telling himself. He needed to get this shit all straightened out fast. Even if the security system had laser beams and snipers, it might not stop her from being hurt in an attack.

"I have to make a few calls." His eyes wandered over her; most of her was covered up, but her shapely legs weren't, and the thin material of the t-shirt didn't do much to hide the peaks of her perfectly shaped nipples. Between worrying about the Stephanos family and wanting to get his dick inside of her, he wasn't entirely sure his heart would hold out.

"If my dad knew where I was the whole time, why didn't he just come for me himself? I mean, he called like twice, but then nothing. Then you showed up."

He ran his fingers through his hair. "I don't know. I wondered that myself, but wasn't given much of an answer when I tried to ask." In fact, the whole damn situation had been thrust on him with too little information.

Pain, the wounded look of a child being rejected, passed through her features. It was brief, but still he saw it and could identify it in a heartbeat. He'd worn the same expression for years as a kid. Devin and his mom had done what they could to shield him, and he never let on that he knew more than they thought, but he knew damn well his father had walked out without giving a shit about them.

"I'm going to shower. Can I use your phone to call her back, so she knows I'm okay?"

"No. No more contact with anyone back home. If Jesse goes back there, it's better your friends don't know anything."

"But Charity and Jackson are going to be worried," she insisted, her pain quickly turning into anger. He knew that trick, too. But it'd been years since he'd employed it. It had never served him well when he did.

"They'll be fine. How are your hands?" He approached her, picking up her hands and inspecting the palms.

"Just a little sore." She'd already taken off the bandages. The dark red lines crossing both palms looked clean and were starting to heal.

"Yeah. They'll be sore for a while." He dropped her hands. "You might have trouble with the shower, I can help with that." Imagining helping her out of that oversized shirt to reveal her breasts beneath already had him hard. Telling himself to think of something else only led to him remembering how sweet it had been to spread apart her creamy white thighs and fuck her so hard he nearly lost himself in his orgasm.

As if on instinct, knowing how much he wanted to grab her and toss her over the edge of the couch, she stepped away.

"I think I can manage." She flashed a soft smile and turned toward the stairs.

He didn't miss the way her hips swayed a bit more than usual while she walked, or the little peek she gave to see if he was watching. If there had been a gorilla standing in the room, Trevor wouldn't have even noticed.

Once she disappeared, he let out a breath. Shit, the woman was getting to him. It had to stop. She was just the girl he was watching. No big deal. Once everything was straight, she'd go home, he'd go back to the precinct, and everything would go back to normal.

The ringing of his cell finally got his attention off the stairs and trying to see through walls as she took off her clothes and readied for the shower.

"Hello."

"Detective Stringer, where's my daughter?"

ADDISON SHOWERED QUICKLY. Not because she was in any hurry really, she had nowhere to be, but it was habit. The faster she could ready herself in the morning, the longer she could sleep in. A fair trade-off, she always figured, even if it meant she wouldn't have time to flat iron the waves from her hair.

She hadn't taken the time to take a proper inventory for what she would need on the run with Trevor, so she hadn't bothered to pack her hair dryer or her flat iron. Her hair would be an unruly mess if she didn't tame it with at least a hair dryer. The curls would kink up into tight twists, and she'd look more poodle than adult woman.

"He's got to have something around here. Even men use a hair dryer," she muttered to herself while digging through the cabinets in the bathroom. Not a stranger to the finer things, even she was envious of the marble tiling, the Jacuzzi tub, and the impressive overhead lighting the bathroom had to offer.

After rummaging around, she struck gold and pulled out the outdated dryer; after scrounging around for a comb, she looked almost presentable.

Although why she felt the need to go to any trouble at all made little sense to her. She was just with Trevor, and he'd already seen her in her pajamas looking all battered from sleep. It didn't sit right, finding herself attracted to him. Not that she hadn't met her fair share of hot men, but he was different. There was a quality she didn't see often. Unshakable. Nothing seemed to faze him or throw him off guard. He came across as very matter of fact, but she'd expect nothing less from a cop, but not unwilling to change directions when needed. He gave the impression of being somewhat laid back, but the way he'd wielded that damn belt the morning before had shattered that idea. Steven never spanked her that hard, or that long. Most of her punishments were over shortly after they started and almost always ended up with makeup sex.

Once she was dressed in a clean shirt and jeans, she embarked on going back downstairs. Maybe she could convince him to let her fire up the laptop she'd noticed in the office next to the bedroom and send an email.

"Of course, I understand, Sir. I assure you, your daughter will be kept safe and brought home to you just as soon as possible." Trevor's voice carried throughout the lower level and up the stairs.

She froze before she hit the landing where he could see her.

"If you have any information on the Stephanos family trying to get to her at the club, that would be helpful... uh huh... of course, Sir. I'll have her home as quickly as I can."

She grabbed the railing to steady herself. How could she have thought he was trustworthy? He was a cop, wasn't he? Hadn't her father taught her that much about life? Everything had a price, everyone could be bought. Trevor was no different.

Craning her neck, she peered around the corner toward the kitchen where he stood with his back to her. He'd gone silent; her father probably ranting on the other end. If she didn't hate him at that moment, she'd feel sorry for him. But he made his bed, he and her father could snuggle up together under the fucking blankets for all she cared. She was not going back to Chicago. She was not marrying Jesse Stephanos and that was that.

Sighting his keys on the end table close to the front door, she eyed the distance from where he was to the door. He'd left the car parked in front of the house.

Using all the stealth she possessed, she made her way to the door, thankful her gym shoes were broken in enough they made no sound as they padded across the marble flooring. Seriously, who had such a beautiful house in the middle of the damn woods?

Just as she reached the end table, Trevor turned around, catching her gaze instantly. She gulped and held still for a moment. He was talking into the phone, but she wasn't hearing anything, only watching him as though if she moved too quickly he'd know what her plan was and would pounce.

His brow wrinkled when she didn't move away from the table.

"I'll have to call you back," he said into his phone. She didn't wait; the moment was already slipping away. She snatched the keys, threw the lock, and yanked the door open.

Her feet beat down the stairs as she pummeled her

way to the car. She heard her name being called, heard him order her to stop, to get back in the house.

No way.

A loose piece of gravel on the drive tripped her up, and she nearly face planted. Losing more time than acceptable to right herself again, she pushed herself harder.

"I swear if you open that door you're going to regret it, Addison!" His roar was close, too damn close.

She started fumbling with the keys, pressing buttons trying to unlock the stupid sedan. Finally, the car beeped, and she gripped the handle.

"Last chance, Addison," he yelled, but he was only a few feet away. She could feel him behind her, but she didn't want to look. If she looked, and he had that face —that angry, but calm face—she might relent. And she had to get away. He was going to take her back to her father, and that couldn't happen.

"Fuck you!" She yanked the door, nearly falling on her ass when it swung open, and she scrambled to get in the car. She got it closed and locked just as he showed up at the window. She didn't dare look at him. Instead she fiddled with the keys looking for the one for the ignition.

"Addison." A calm voice called through the window.

She continued to ignore him. Finding a key that looked right, she started to insert it into the ignition.

Nothing there. She growled and started to look at the console. No fucking ignition.

"Uh, Addison." He wrapped his knuckles on the window again. With a loud grunt, she looked out the window. From his middle finger dangled a black square. The car was keyless. No key for the ignition. "Open the door. Now."

She pulled up her virtual big girl panties and met his eyes. Not doing that had been the right call the first time. His eyes were narrowed, but dark as night. The amount of pressure in which he was pressing his lips together would probably leave them bruised.

An idea struck and without thinking, she pressed down on the brake and pushed the ignition button. The car sputtered a bit, then roared to life. She cheered and jostled in her seat to get comfortable. He'd been close enough to get it going, but how far could it go without him in the car?

She never had a chance to find out. The car beeped, and the door swung open. A large hand snatched her arm and yanked her out of the car. She would have fallen to her knees if he hadn't bent down to hoist her over his shoulder. Two hard smacks to her ass and he kicked the door shut.

"No!" She pounded on his back. "Trevor! No! Dammit!"

"You already have a washing coming, and a whoopin'; keep it up and I'll add the cane. I like the cane. So many little crevices it can reach." The man wasn't even out of breath as he carried her squirming body back up the stairs and into the house.

"Put me down!" She kicked her legs and tried to get a hold of his boxers to yank them up. Maybe wedging his underwear up his ass would get him to relent and put her down. Except he apparently hadn't bothered with any that morning. Animal.

"Sure will, just as soon as we get there." He didn't head up the stairs, instead he carried her down a long hallway. She tried to grab onto the walls, to slow him at least, but all she managed to do was break a few nails.

"Where are you taking me?" she demanded between blows to his back.

"Blake has a home dungeon," he said, as though he'd just told her Blake had a wine rack.

"I don't want to go there now. I'm not in the mood." She stilled in her hitting him.

"I'm sure you don't," he laughed. "You sure as hell won't want to stay once I get you there. But you're the one who went all runaway on me."

Hearing a key pad beeping and a door opening, she started to rethink her actions. "You were going to take me home! You promised me you wouldn't, but you told my dad you were!"

He didn't stop to have a conversation, he simply walked inside, shut the door and finally released her, dropping her to the floor. She landed in a huddled mess at his feet.

"Stay down there." He shoved her with his bare foot when she tried to scramble up to her feet. "Get on your knees."

"Trevor—"

"I promise, you'll want to start using the right words real quick, sweet-cheeks." Although the words suggested he was teasing, the tone in which he said them did not. "Knees. Now."

Slowly, she eased herself onto her knees, pressing her ass back against her heels, in case he got the idea of swatting her again.

He squatted down in front of her, taking her chin between his thumb and forefinger. "I told you I'm going to help you figure out what exactly all happened, and to find a way to get you home safe. And that's what I'm doing. If I told your father what we were actually doing, do you think he'd send me his blessing?"

She swallowed. Okay, he had a point. But, how was she supposed to know that? Everyone having anything to do with her father betrayed her to stay in his good graces. Why would she think Trevor was different?

Because he was, and somewhere in the deep recesses of her mind and her body, she knew that. And instead of asking him about the conversation, or giving him a moment to explain, she'd run, tried to steal his car.

"I-I thought—"

"You thought the worst, because it's what you're used to seeing when it comes to your dad. I get that." He released her chin. "You jumped to the wrong conclusion, you didn't even give me a chance, and you fucking tried to steal my car!"

"I'm sorry." She lifted her chin when he stood up.

"I've heard that before." He crossed his arms over his chest. "Do you see this room?" He jerked his chin, indicating she should look around.

When she did, her breath caught in her throat. To anyone outside the lifestyle it would resemble a torture chamber from the middle ages. A St. Andrews cross, a spanking bench, a chained spider web, and hooks embedded in the walls all over the place. On one wall hung several implements. Not a handful, but several of each type. Five different paddles, three floggers, two riding crops, and more coiled whips than she wanted to count.

"Blake loves whips. Doesn't use them on his subs though, he just likes the sound to set the mood."

She swallowed hard, forcing herself to bring her eyes back to him.

"And you?"

He huffed. "Me? Not a whip guy. Never could wield it right, but the flogger, the paddle, the cane? Hell, you'll be able to tell me what you think shortly enough."

"Trevor—" Her mouth dried at the casual grin curling on his lips. He was enjoying this, toying with her fear.

"The door has a keypad on it. That's how it locks. From inside, there's another keypad." He twisted to point it out next to the door. "Blake owns the place, but his brother visits from time to time, and he doesn't let him in here." Trevor shrugged. "You'll stay in here until I'm ready for you. I'm a little pissed at the moment, and I never punish when I'm pissed, but make no fucking mistake, you are in for one hell of a punishment."

"No." She shook her head. "I was only trying to protect myself." When she started to rise, he shoved her back down with one hand, bringing his face down to hers, nose to nose.

"You have me for that, sweet-cheeks. That's my job now. And it's also my job to make sure you obey, because if you don't obey me, how can I save you? How can I protect someone who runs off halfcocked?"

She let out a long breath, but he didn't move, didn't even flinch.

"How can I?"

He wanted an answer? "I didn't go off halfcocked."

He snorted. "No? Okay, then, what were you going to do when you got to the end of the road? Go right or left? And the next one? And the next? Because these roads are all winding. One wrong turn and you'll be deeper in the woods than you probably ever stepped foot. And if you did get to the main road, what then? You have no money for gas, your phones busted up so no calling for help, and you left all your clothes here."

She closed her eyes for a second, trying to shut out his logic.

"See. Sounds halfcocked to me." He stood back to his full height. "Get comfortable. And by comfortable, I mean naked. I think you've had enough clothing for a while." He winked and headed toward the door.

"You can't leave me in here! What if there's a fire?"

"If there's a fire outside the room, you're fine, the room was built like a damn bunker. If the fire starts in here, well, for one I'd like to know how you managed that, and two, there's an intercom over there that plays into all the rooms."

She wanted to sprint out of the room once he opened the door, but her legs were glued in place by her own self admission of guilt.

"And, if you use the intercom there better be something really wrong. Got me?"

He didn't even wait for her to answer before he shut the door. A few beeps and the bolt slid in place. She was locked in, caged by the person who was supposed to be helping her.

11

The banging finally stopped. It took nearly twenty minutes for her to realize kicking the steel door wasn't going to get her anywhere.

Trevor leaned against the wall staring at the barrier standing between him and the naughty girl who'd actually tried to steal his car. His own car, the one he'd used to save her ass, not once but twice from the Stephanos boys.

He could understand her desperation to keep from going back to her father. The bastard had a special talent for creeping him out. His desire to have his daughter home didn't stem from a fatherly love or concern. There was almost as much desperation in him to get his hands on her as there was for her to stay out of his clutches.

That didn't excuse her behavior though. Trying to

run away was grounds for punishment in his book; grand theft auto compounded that sentence.

But it was more than that that had gotten his blood hot. At least he could admit that to himself. She didn't believe he was helping her. The girl actually thought he was going to bring her home to Daddy even after he promised to do the exact opposite of that. He'd given his word. No matter what she thought she heard on his call, she should have given him the benefit of the doubt. To at least ask him a fucking question before bolting like he was some mass murdering captor.

He wouldn't deny there were cops in the city who were on someone's payroll. But not him. Never him. For that stigma to still stick to him even after everything he did to get away from that shit made his skin feel too tight for his body. She didn't know, couldn't know, but she'd assumed. Jumped right to that decision; he was a dirty cop.

Growling at old ghosts, he strode to the door. The longer he waited, the more irritated he became. Better to deal with her, so he could get on with helping her and not have to worry she'd take off again. The last thing he needed was to have to run through the fucking woods trying to track her down. He'd find her, that wasn't a question, but it would waste time. And from what he'd gathered from his conversation with dear old Dad, time wasn't a luxury either of them had.

He punched in the key code to the playroom, trying to remember the last girl he'd brought up to the cabin for some weekend fun. Brittany? Bethany? Something with a B and she'd not been as thrilled as he thought she'd be when she'd seen it. Some girls liked the idea of his sort of play, his demand for obedience, but once faced with it tucked tail. He had a hunch his Addison wasn't that girl.

His Addison? He had to stop that thinking, right the fuck now. She was only his for a short duration, his temporary Addison. There. Better, though why it left a sour taste in his mouth wasn't something he was going to pick apart just yet.

Prepared to have her hurl herself at him when the door opened, he was surprised to find her standing naked in the center of the room. Her hair disheveled from her little fit of anger, and her chest rising and falling at a rapid pace. It wasn't chilly in the room, but her nipples were hard peaks, jutting out from her breasts. He took a long moment to get a good look at her; fuck, she was gorgeous. Her hands fidgeted her sides, but she didn't cover herself. Point to her for that, good girl.

"Kneel." He shut the door and set the lock. He wasn't expecting any trouble from either outside or inside the room, but being safe never made him sorry.

Leaves falling from the maple trees outside in the fall breeze had less grace than Addison as she moved to her knees. Her hands went behind her back, her eyes downcast on the floor. Being reminded that someone had taught her that position, and that someone hadn't been him, did little to ease his irritated state.

"No. Your hands go on your thighs." He liked them behind her back, but that was someone else's position, not for him to use, and sure as fuck not for her to use with him.

She gave a little nod and slid her palms down her legs until they rested just above her knees. Her eyes were still downcast.

"I'm sorry I tried to run away." Her soft voice portrayed exactly the correct amount of remorse. He folded his arms over his chest and waited for the rest. She didn't wait long. "I was just afraid. I'm sure you get that."

How many times had her sweetness gotten her out of a good licking in the past? "I do. I also get that you tried to steal my car, and when I called you back, you didn't come. I also get that even when I was standing right there at the car you still tried to get it to turn on and go. It's a keyless car, Addison. You might have gotten it to start, you may have even gotten to the end of the drive, but what then?" He had no real idea if the car would simply shut off without the signal from his key, but he doubted she did either.

"I'm sorry. I'll accept whatever punishment you see

fit." Oh, there it was. The sweet surrender of martyred submission. Accepting a punishment was one thing, and something he usually found erotic, but this wasn't that. This was her manipulating him, trying to show him a side of her that wasn't real. And Addison was the real thing.

He prowled the room, walking around her, never taking his eyes off of her.

"You ran because you were scared. What will you do the next time you're frightened?"

Her lips, those fuckable, kissable lips, parted but nothing came out. Didn't really have a plan, this one.

"I'll talk to you about it." Fair enough, still full of bullshit, but that's fine. He could work with that.

"So, you saw me on the phone with your dad. Heard me assure him I'd get you home, which I will, just not the way he wants, and you're afraid, what would you do now?" He stopped in front of her, waiting for her to look up at him. She didn't.

"If I heard you having that conversation again, I'd ask you about it. I would tell you about being afraid."

He laughed. Her eyes shot up to his. "Sorry, sweet-cheeks. You're full of a lot right now, but remorse and repentance isn't it. I believe you might actually ask me about the call, maybe, but I'm not certain. I am positive you wouldn't come to me with your fears."

Her nostrils flared, not exaggerated like some wolf

getting ready to pounce, but a subtle movement from a girl trying to hide her anger.

"I already apologized." Her voice hardened.

"Yeah, and I already said you're getting punished." He shrugged one shoulder. His hands itched to touch her, spank her, fuck her, but he had to rein himself in. One of them needed to be in control, and it wasn't her, much to her irritation, he gathered.

"Trevor."

"So, you're the top from the bottom type," he announced, and anger flashed in her eyes.

"We aren't playing," she shot at him. Such attitude for a naked girl on her knees before him. A spirit lived in her that would be a shame to kill; taming it would be the adventure he'd choose.

"No. We aren't. But you are still trying to control what happens in this room. You still think if you bat your eyelashes, say you're sorry, and come up with some bullshit that you'll get out of what you have coming. That doesn't work with me, sweet-cheeks. And if it worked in the past, I'm sorry for it. Because this will be so much harder for you to take."

Her throat worked as she swallowed hard. "This is stupid." She shot to her feet before he could stop her. "I'm not your submissive. This is such a fucked-up game. Either help me or don't, but I'm not playing this fucking game with you anymore."

The door was locked. She wasn't going anywhere,

so he didn't chase her. He wouldn't do that, not again. She'd come back to him willingly and ready or they'd be standing there for a while.

She tugged on the door, and he rolled his eyes. The woman's emotions ruled her actions. If she'd take a second to think before her little outburst she'd remember the door was locked.

"Let me out."

"No."

She turned to him, eyes narrowed and hands on her hips. "I'm not playing around, Trevor. I'm not letting you punish me. This is a stupid game that means nothing, so just let me out."

She hadn't said her safeword. No way he was opening that door. "Nope." He shook his head. "I'm not doing that. What is going to happen is you're going to get back on your fucking knees, you're going to crawl over here, and you're going to take off my belt for me, kiss it, and ask me to begin your punishment."

Her right foot stomped hard onto the floor, sending ripples through her body and making her breasts bounce. For that fact alone he didn't chastise her for the act.

"I will not."

"Then we are going to be here a while. But I'll warn you, the longer it takes, the more you'll earn. Right now, you have a belting and a paddling coming, not to mention the mouth washing, and a few other tricks I have up my sleeve to make sure this little fit of yours never returns." He wouldn't force her, and if she said her word, he'd unlock the door and let her out. He'd hate it, but he'd make himself do it.

"I don't like this game." Genuine softness edged its way into her voice. Her hands went limp at her sides, and the fire died in her eyes.

"It's not a game." Not to him anyway. "I take obedience seriously, and yeah, we aren't a couple. But for right now, you're under my protection, which makes you fall under my rules, and my authority."

Not a couple. That sentence, though true, didn't feel right, and from the sag of her shoulders he didn't think she liked it either. He dragged his hand through his hair.

"Now. Get on your knees, crawl here, and do what I said. Do it now, before I stop being so generous with you." He dropped his arms to his sides, and waited.

For the second time that morning, he watched her ease onto her knees. This time, she dropped to her hands as well and began to crawl. He tried to ignore the sway of her breasts, and the way her hips moved with each step. He forced himself to remember there was a long road before he could get his cock back inside of her, but his body didn't give a shit. The woman, even when looking as downtrodden as she was at that moment, was fucking beautiful.

When she approached him, she pushed herself up

to her knees and reached for his belt. He moved his hands to his back, letting her have free rein. He kept his eyes on her, watching every little tick in her cheek. Her tongue darted out to lick her lips when the belt buckle got stuck. The jangle of the buckle and the yank of the leather through his loops didn't distract him at all from the determination in her gaze.

"Addison." He covered her hands with his until she looked up at him. He searched for fear in her expression, or repulsion or anger, something that would tell him to give up this stupid idea of claiming her, but he found nothing. He found relief. She'd pushed him, but he didn't topple over. She wanted his strength, and he was going to give it to her. "Make sure you kiss the belt that's going to mark your ass before you hand it to me."

MASTER. The word tingled the tip of her tongue. She could say it, and he would honor it. Hell, maybe he would even still help her with her father and the Stephanos problem. But did she really want that? Did she want a completely platonic equal existence with him until that time?

He'd said it wasn't a game to him, and she could sense it wasn't just the current situation he was referring to. One uttered word and she could stand back up, dress herself, and be let out of the playroom. Having that option made it safe not to use it.

She loved the smell of leather, and the scent of his brown well-worn belt was no different. As she drew the strap through her hands, folding in half and bringing it to her lips, she inhaled. A moment of pleasure before he brought down his wrath.

He had a casual expression, like he was waiting for his coffee, but his fingers were rubbing together at his sides. Punishment or not, he was getting off on her submission, the steel rod pressing against his zipper proved it. Wanting him to fuck her, even though he'd just promised her a hell of a spanking, was messed up. She knew it, but there wasn't much she could do about it. Her pussy was already getting wet, just from kneeling in front of him. Kissing his belt and offering it to him only made that situation worse.

He took the belt from her hands when she lifted it up to him, rubbing the folded loop along her jaw. "Good. Now you see that spanking bench? Get your ass over it, raise it up for me, offer it to me. When you're ready, you'll ask me to begin."

A pang in her chest caught her off guard. She'd never had to ask for a punishment before. If it weren't happening to her, she might find the idea appealing; a little humiliation play now and then was good for her libido. But it *was* happening to her, and it wasn't play, it was real.

When she started to stand, he tsked his tongue and pressed his bare foot against her shoulder to keep her down. Without even giving a verbal command, he pointed to the bench.

Resolved to get through this with her dignity intact, she moved on all fours, crawling to the bench. She didn't need to look behind her to know his eyes were on her ass. The little sashay wasn't easy to do on all fours, but she made do. After all, why should she be the only one who was uncomfortable?

Once at the bench she moved to her feet and climbed on. She'd played on plenty of benches to know what position was the most comfortable. Thankfully this particular model had hand grips. She pressed her knees into the padded leather and bent over to grab the handles.

"Arch your back more." He tapped her ass with the belt.

She rolled her eyes and did as he instructed, knowing he could now see everything her body had to offer. The leather gifted a cool reprieve to her heated face as she finished getting into position. Her sex was wet; he had to see the juices on her lips. As though he needed any further encouragement to tease her.

"I wouldn't keep me waiting too much longer." The dark warning cut through her anticipation.

"Trevor, will you please begin my punishment."

The tips of his fingers trailed up her thigh to her

rounded cheeks then down the other thigh. "Of course. Tell me why you're being punished. What naughty thing did you do this time to warrant such a hard punishment?"

She swallowed and clenched her eyes closed. "I assumed the worst and tried to run away. I tried to steal your car."

"Yes, and there's the not listening when I called you, the hitting me when I picked you up, the kicking and squirming when I got you in here. The kicking the door when I very clearly told you to undress and kneel. Oh. And the cursing. I've lost count on how many times."

She sighed. Not awake even a full hour and she'd made a real mess of things. "Yes, Sir," she whispered, having nothing else to say.

The leather snapped against his palm. "I guess we can get started then."

She tried to get a grip on her panic. He'd gone easy on her the first time, and she'd been able to count on him holding her while he spanked her over his lap. She wasn't tied down, he wasn't holding her in place. If she jumped up, broke position, it would be her fault. Having to simply take what he was going to give her made it worse.

"Keep your hands out of my way. If you get up before I give you permission, there'll be extra."

She nodded, unable to speak. What the hell had

she gotten herself into? Her ass clenched, her body tensed, waiting for the first strike.

"No, soften your ass. I want your cheeks soft. Good, like that." He stroked her again with his fingertips. She shuddered when his fingers went away, missing the touch immediately.

His large hand clapped down on the underside of her bottom, jolting her with surprise. Another slap and then another peppered her, not missing a spot. She grunted from the impact, but it didn't hurt, not in comparison for what was coming once he was done with his preparation.

"There, nice and pink." He gave her another half dozen swats. One last smack, and he gripped her cheek, squeezing until she squirmed from the sharp pinch of his fingers. "Ready for the belting?"

She nodded but he gave her a quick slap to her thigh.

"Unless you have rocks in your head, I can't hear when you shake it. And I know for a fact you don't have rocks in that pretty head of yours."

"Yes, I'm ready." She groaned when he pinched her again. Her foot wanted to kick out at him, to get him away from her already warm bottom, but lucky for her, her mind kept her body in check. For the time being, at least.

"You aren't going to move, sweet-cheeks. You're going to take all ten of these licks. You can yell if you need, and you can cry, but you will not curse, and you will not kick me." Even though his warning sounded gruff, the soft pat of his hand on her butt reminded her he didn't need to be feared. Oh, he was going to hurt her, there was no getting around that, but he wouldn't harm her. And that made all the difference.

"Yes, Sir." She swallowed and adjusted her grip on the handles, readying herself. The belt jangled, a minute sound really, right before it struck across both cheeks. She clenched her teeth, her body tightened beneath the heated lash.

"Soft," he ordered, tapping her ass again. Another blazing strap landed just below the first once she complied. "If I have to tell you each time, I'll go harder." Harder? Two stripes and her ass was already on fire.

"I'll try." It was the only promise she could give.

Trevor swung the belt again, striking her just below the first two, and getting dangerously close to her sit spot. The next three lashes came fast, hard, and right over the curve of her ass. When he didn't like her arch, he forced her ass out further again, landing a hard blow in just the right spot to get her pussy. She howled and bit down on her lip. No cursing was worse than not being able to jump up. But he probably knew that.

She'd lost count of the strikes, and was beyond relieved when he finally dropped the belt onto her back. "Hold that for me, babe," he joked. She took deep gulping breaths while he walked away.

Tears brimmed in her eyes, her lungs heated from all the air she'd swallowed and the crying. She'd never screamed out before during a spanking. The man was relentless. Steven would have stopped at the first sign of real tears, at real discomfort, but not Trevor. He had a lesson he wanted to drive home, and they wouldn't be done until he was sure he'd accomplished it.

"Just three with the paddle," he announced, plucking something off that wall she'd seen. Knowing it wouldn't make it any easier to see the offending implement, she didn't bother to turn to look.

She nodded, her forehead sliding against the now slick leather of the bench.

He rubbed her throbbing backside with the paddle. Wood. It felt like wood, smooth and polished. She hated wood.

"Almost there, babe. You can do this for me, right? You can take your punishment for me? You were a bad girl, but you'll be good for me now, right?" The paddle continued to roam over her ass. Her answer was apparently a requirement.

"Yes. Yes, Sir," she sniffled. Wiping the tears from her face, she re-gripped the bars; the pain from the burns became secondary to the inferno happening on her backside.

His hand flattened on her back, sending a current

of reassurance through her body. The paddle pulled back from her body, leaving a cooling sensation just before it landed square over both cheeks. She screamed out and bucked up, but his hand pressed her back down. He delivered the second strike directly in the same spot, and she shook her head, yelling out again and trying to wiggle away.

"It's worse! It's worse!" she yelled when the paddle pressed against her backside, preparing for the last strike. Without a word, he pulled back and unleashed the hardest strike yet, pushing her forward on the bench. Her body tensed and released and every tear she ever fought against burst from her eyes.

Hard sobs racked her body. Tears pooled on the leather bench beneath her, and she didn't care.

He didn't walk away, he didn't leave her; instead his hands caressed her, running down her back, up her thighs but completely avoiding her hot and swollen globes.

She didn't know where the paddle went or if the belt was still on her back. After long minutes passed, he eased her up off the bench and wrapped his arms around her shoulders, pulling her to his chest and kissing her wet cheeks. The sobbing finally stopped, but the tears were still falling.

"I think we broke the dam." He gave her a reas-suring smile and ran his thumbs across both cheeks.

She nodded. It has been so long since she cried,

really cried. She really gave in and let her emotions expand until they took over her body in such a way. The tears she'd given him back at the motel couldn't compare to the torrential downpour of sobs he'd just pulled from her with his discipline.

He kissed her forehead, then her nose and her cheeks. "C'mon, sweet-cheeks." Bending down, he scooped her up into his arms. Her arms snaked around his neck and she sucked in air when his arm brushed her throbbing ass. "Not sorry about that." He snuggled her closer to him and went to the door, punching in the key code and unlocking it. Her eyelids fell; no amount of will power could keep them open as he made their way through the house. She heard his footsteps on the stairs, felt herself being lowered onto cool sheets, but other than rolling onto her stomach to avoid anything touching her ass, she wasn't participating in anything. She needed and wanted sleep.

12

The last time he'd punished his submissive that hard had been the last time he'd seen Carolina. Not that she hadn't deserved it, driving drunk was a big no-no to him, and lying about it afterward, fuck no. She'd taken her punishment like a big girl, but afterward, she'd bowed out, telling him she didn't want to answer to anyone. She wanted full independence and only wanted to submit in bed. She'd been fine with the rules and light punishments, but the first time the discipline got real, she'd wanted out.

Addison wouldn't have that option. She could pause a spanking with her safeword, even stop the action altogether, but she wasn't going anywhere. Not if he could help it. He was an asshole for it, he knew that. The fact didn't bother him. And between his belt and that wicked oak paddle he found in the playroom, he could be sure she wouldn't step foot out that fucking door again without asking permission.

They most likely had a day, two at the most, before her father forced him into action, and the detectives he reached out to weren't getting back to him yet. They would; he trusted Blake and if they were solid for Blake, that was enough for Trevor.

Dragging his hands through his wet hair for the third time, he went in search of something to wear. Blake kept extra clothes in the cabin, and hopefully he would find something that didn't resemble Paul Bunyan.

As he passed the room Addison slept in, he decided to peek in on her. They weren't finished with her discipline, but she'd needed the break. And truth be told so did he. Her squirms and her cries tore at him and stroked him at the same time. Every sob he heard, every tear he'd seen warred within him. He wanted to fuck her so hard that her cries became groans of ecstasy, and her cries of pain became mingled with pleasure. Scooping her up and carrying her to bed had saved them both from him going back on his word. He still had punishment to deliver, but until his mind cleared he wasn't doing it.

She wasn't sleeping. She lay on her side, the blanket pushed down past her ass. Red stripes from the belt still covered her cheeks, and large splatters of a deeper red indicated where the paddle had struck. She glanced at the door. Her red puffy eyes stilled on him.

"You're up," he stated the obvious and pushed the door open.

She shifted in the bed, pulling the cover up over her still naked body.

"You think the blanket will protect you from me?" He laughed, but didn't push her. Instead he plopped down in the armchair near the window, studying her.

"Do you have any cream?" she asked, leaning up on her elbow and tucking her hair behind her ears.

"For what?"

"Me. My—" She waved her hand behind her to indicate she meant her ass.

"Like arnica cream?" he snorted. "No. I mean maybe, Blake might have some around here, but none for naughty girls." He shook his finger at her. "It's really a nice day outside." With one finger, he brushed away the curtain to look out into the surrounding woods.

"I assume I won't be going out there," she breathed and rested her head back on the pillow.

"Uh, correct." He decided she'd had enough rest. "You won't be, at least not until you've gone through the rest of your punishment."

Her ears perked at that, and he forced himself not to laugh at the shock on her expression. "Remind me what part we still have to take care of." He stood and shoved his hands into his jeans. She eyed him hovering, and aside from the arousal he took immediate note of, she looked wary. "You need to understand that when I say something, I mean it. If I say you'll be punished, you will be; we had this discussion already."

"I didn't argue." She closed her eyes and draped her arm over them.

"You aren't taking this seriously."

"Trevor, I've been punished enough already."

"You decided that? You made the decision that your punishment is over?" He lowered his voice and steadied himself. She would need to stop fighting him at every turn. He could see the submissiveness inside of her. She knew it was there, but she'd never truly tapped into it. Not all of it. She skimmed the surface and when it got too hairy she backed off, but she wouldn't with him. She would give him everything.

Her brown eyes peeked out at him from under her arm. "What time is it?"

Change the subject. Not very creative of her.

"Time to get up. Now, tell me what we have left to deal with."

She huffed, and moved her arm to cover her eyes again. "You said a mouth washing, and some other tricks or something." He grinned down at her. If she only knew what would come to her if she started to behave, she'd stop trying to push away so much. She'd start obeying a hell of a lot quicker. Hopefully he'd get to show her how he treated his good girl. But first the naughty one needed tending to.

"A think a good wash everywhere will do nicely. I'll get the bath ready, meet me in the bathroom." He didn't wait for a response. Other than obedience, there wasn't one that would interest him anyway.

Blake wasn't a small man by any means, which meant a standard size bathtub would be useless for him. Thankfully, the large Jacuzzi tub came with two chrome-finished faucets to help fill it faster. By the time Addison slipped into the room, the water level had risen enough for him to turn off the water.

Still sporting a bit of bedhead, she leaned against the counter with her arms folded over her belly. Some men might drool over a flat stomach with toned muscles; his tastes ran a little more realistic. While other women might try hiding their naked breasts, or their bare pussies, Addison tried to cover the small pouch of her stomach. Society really did a number on women and their bodies. Such a shame.

"Put your hands down at your sides." He stood up from the ledge of the tub and moved to stand in front of her. Keeping her eyes anywhere near his, she did as she was told, though the new blush in her cheeks relayed her dislike for the dictate. "You have a gorgeous body, and I won't let you hide even an inch of it from me. I could leave you completely naked at all times, to get the lesson across. Would that make it easier for you?"

Her eyes shot up to his, and she shook her head. "No." Blinking a few times, she started again. "No, you don't have to do that."

He gave a nod and brushed her hair back over her shoulders. "Well, that sort of sucks for me really, but if you think you can keep from hiding your body from me when you're naked, then I won't take away your clothes."

"It's not that I have body issues. I mean, I'm not one of those women who hates her body and needs you to fix that."

Now she had his attention. "That's good to hear."

"It's just you're so fit and toned, and obviously spend hours in a gym." The blush intensified and her gaze dropped. "And well, I've never even been inside of a gym."

"If I wanted you to start working out, told you that you needed to get toned and ripped for me, would you? And not for health reasons—because for health reasons everyone should at least have some activity—but I mean for appearance's sake. Would you do it?"

Her chin lifted, and her shoulders squared off. "No. Not for appearance. No."

"For health?" he prodded.

"Health reasons are different, and it would depend

on what restrictions or routine was being put in place."

"And you think that you would have a say? You'd get to be heard?" His fingertip trailed over her collarbone, but she kept her focus on his face.

"Yes." She didn't sound as confident as she had a minute ago, but she took a small breath and continued. "If I was in a real relationship, one that was headed for long term, then yes. Because I wouldn't be in that relationship with someone who thought he could just micromanage or walk all over me. I'm submissive, not stupid."

He didn't waste time telling her how much he loved her answer. His hand wrapped behind her neck, and he brought his mouth over hers. Her hands came up and rested against his chest, gripping his shirt while he deepened the kiss. Her lips parted the moment his tongue touched them, and he swooped in. Craving her taste, her sensations, he wanted to possess everything about her at that moment.

Some subs didn't get it. They couldn't grasp their own power in the relationship, but not Addison. There was no denying her worth and her strength. She wasn't someone to crumble beneath his domination. No, she would blossom and thrive beneath it.

When he pulled away from the kiss, running his tongue over her bottom lip one last time, he pressed his forehead to hers. "Sweet-cheeks, you make it hard to punish you when you show me how perfect you are."

The muscles in her neck tensed beneath his hand. Going back now wouldn't help either of them; they would both be left with an empty sensation if he went back on his word.

Her lips curled. She may think she wanted out, but he knew better.

"I said you make it hard, not impossible. Do you need to pee before you get in the tub for your washing?"

WELL, didn't he know exactly how to ruin a wonderful moment? Addison stepped away from him and did her best not glare at him too hard. Obviously in the punishing mindset, she didn't need to push him further in that direction.

"Can I have a minute?" She glanced over at the toilet, looming in the room.

"Sure." He shrugged and sat back down on the ledge.

"No, I mean alone."

"Oh, then no." He smiled. Actually smiled, a deliciously handsome smile right up at her. Her lips still tingled from his kiss, and with that grin of his, she wanted another. But she wanted to pee more. And she wanted to do it alone.

"Trevor, can't you give just a little?"

"Nope. Until your punishment is over, you get no privacy, no leniency, and really have no right to ask for anything." Still the smile sat on his lips, not even the harshness of his sentence could take away from his attraction.

She heaved a sigh and padded over to the toilet. "Can you at least not look?"

He chuckled. "Didn't I just say no right to ask for anything?"

"You should have just finished the punishment then instead of letting me nap," she snapped at him and sat on the toilet. "This prolonged punishment crap is... well... crap." She looked away from him and shut her eyes. If she pretended hard enough that he wasn't there, she could get the act over with and keep her dignity.

Thankfully, he remained silent while she finished and flushed. She ignored him as she went about washing her hands and drying them on the towel hanging nearby. After catching a glimpse of herself in the mirror she winced. Her hair was all over the place.

"Get in the tub," he announced from behind her. "Stay standing though."

She resolved herself to get through whatever stupid act he wanted to put her through and then be done with it all. Nothing he did in the tub could really be as bad as that paddle he'd wielded in the playroom.

He had his back to her as she climbed in the tub. Thank god for small favors, the damn thing was huge and she needed to climb up on the step and over into the tub. There was no possibility of making the climb graceful.

The water was warm, but not enough that she had the urge to sink into it and relax. Though how could she even think of relaxing with him in the room gearing up to punish her some more? Everything she'd done that morning had been wrong, she wouldn't deny that, but she wasn't used to punishments that were more elaborate than a spanking or at worst a caning.

"Things aren't what you're used to, I get that, sweet-cheeks. But my way is the way we are doing things." Trevor voiced her thoughts as he turned around holding a freshly unwrapped bar of soap and a washcloth.

"Swearing is really that big of a deal?" She tried to sound aloof, like the idea of that bar of soap touching the inside of her mouth didn't make her want to gag.

"I've warned you at least half a dozen times about it, more than I should have to. So yeah, it's sort of a big deal to me." If he was joking, he hid it very well.

"Okay, then. I'll try harder." She kept her eyes on

the soap and wondering how horrible it was going to taste.

"Well, that's the hope, but you know—consequences and all that." He stepped to the tub and dipped the bar into the water. She clenched her jaw, thinking she might just say no, not allow it to happen.

She watched with a quickened heart rate as he rubbed the soap over the washcloth, getting it all bubbly. She'd read blogs where subs described being soaped. Their dominants had washed their tongues and the inside of their mouths just like they were cleaning a dish. She swallowed again, preparing for whatever he was going to do.

The bar of soap, still with a few bubbles clinging to the side, appeared before her lips. "Open wide, sweet-cheeks."

She inhaled sharply through her nose; the bar had no fragrance, but she was sure it would have a horrid taste. He didn't command her again, just held the bar in front of her and waited. The only way out was to cry off with her safeword, but she wouldn't do that. Not over soap.

Finally, she parted her lips and was only slightly startled when the bar pushed past her lips and settled into her mouth. "Hold that there," he ordered and let go.

Her teeth clenched the bar. She did her best to keep her tongue away, but it had very little room in which to hide. The cleanser didn't taste as horrible as she anticipated, but it was by no means comfortable. Soon enough spit began to puddle in her mouth, and ooze out the sides of the bar and down her chin.

"Spread your legs." Trevor dipped the washcloth again and began to wash her legs. "Hands folded behind your head." He wasn't even looking at her; he just kept washing her like some invalid.

Her entire body was wet and soapy before he finally turned his attention back to her mouth. "Do you want that out?" he asked, tapping the end of the bar, making it touch her tongue on the inside.

She nodded and inched a little closer to him.

"And your language? Do you think we've cleaned up that problem?"

She nodded again, swishing her tongue to the side, trying desperately to avoid any more contact with the bar.

"No more cursing or disrespectful tones?"

More nodding, but less confidence that she'd be able to keep her tone where he wanted it.

"I'll take it out, but any more foul words out of that pretty mouth of yours and we're right back in here. Got it?" His dark eyes were so focused on her, and hiding all of his thoughts. If he thought the situation humorous she couldn't tell, but he wouldn't laugh at her. He wasn't putting her through this for his amuse-

ment. It was more than that; the man really didn't like
her cursing.

"Okay, then. Open." He had to catch the bar before
it fell into the tub as it flew out of her mouth when she
opened. He did chuckle then. "Guess you really didn't
like it."

She worked her mouth open and closed. "No."

She moved her hand to wipe her mouth, but he
stopped her with a look.

"Please? Can I rinse?" She longed to put her mouth
beneath the nozzle and drown away the taste.

"Not yet." He shook his head and put the bar of
soap on the edge of the tub. "Almost done, but I need
to finish cleaning you, turn around and put your arms
on the wall."

She didn't argue. Better to get it all over with. So
far it wasn't too bad, and really, him touching her
couldn't be a bad thing.

Hands planted on the wall, she arched her back,
giving her ass to him.

He let out a low whistle. "You might have a small
bruise here. I'll stay clear of that cheek until it's all
better." He patted her right butt cheek gently.

Before she could give a retort, his hands spread her
cheeks and the washcloth was being dragged along her
backside. She clenched her eyes and her teeth closed
as she reminded herself that he was almost done.

When he was done with her ass, his fingers traveled lower, through her pussy lips until he found her clit. Even with the humiliation—or because of it—her clit was ready for his touch. She moaned at the light brush of his fingertip, and she arched even further back at him.

"Hmm, you like this?" He rubbed her harder, circling her clit. "I asked a question, sweet-cheeks."

"Yes, Sir." She nodded with no hesitation.

"Of course you do. Discipline, punishment, obedience, all of this turns you on just as much as me. But you have to learn your lessons if you want to get your rewards."

"Please," she whispered, resting her forehead against the cool tiles of the wall.

"You want to come? Your mouth is still full of soap residue; that has to taste nasty. Your naughty ass here still has marks from your spanking earlier. Do you think I should let you come?"

"Please." The only word she could force out of her mouth at the time. His fingers had a way of turning off her vocabulary.

"If you have one, you have to give me three more." His fingers stopped on her clit, pressing down on it but no longer rubbing. Intense pleasure built up, but without movement it sat still.

"Okay." She nodded. She could do that. A blowjob,

some fucking, sure whatever, he could have three orgasms. She just needed the one, right now.

His hand reached around her, cupping her breast as his fingers dived into her body.

"Fuck my hand, sweet-cheeks."

She didn't need much more encouragement after that. She ground her pelvis into his hand while he thrust two fingers into her and continued to brush against her clit.

"Oh, god," she moaned when he began to roll her nipple between his fingers.

"There you go, there's my girl. Fuck my fingers and come hard. I want it to be good, make it good, Addison. Your pussy belongs to me, and I want it to fucking love this."

"Yes, Sir," she groaned. The pressure built up in her clit with each little touch, each word he spoke, it all ramped up higher. "Oh, god, please." She shoved back at him, getting the full impact of his hand against her clit and found herself spiraling.

"That's it, come hard. Come hard for me." He let go of her breasts and gripped her hip, driving harder into her.

The world unleashed in front of her, she screamed out, the walls throwing the sound around the room as wave after wave took her mind and reeled it in circles. Her pussy clamped down, and every pulsation of her orgasm rippled through her body.

When finally, her mind settled back into her body and the waves had ebbed into calm little ripples, she realized his fingers were still rubbing her clit. She jerked her hips, trying to get away, the sensation too good, too powerful against her sensitive nub.

"Nuh-uh, sweet-cheeks. You had one, now you give me three more."

13

Trevor gripped her hip harder, pushing her against the wall of the tub and stepping inside the water. His socks were soaked as well as his jeans, but he didn't give a shit. Extracting the next three from her wasn't going to be easy, she'd fight him, but he'd be disappointed if she didn't.

"No. I can't." She breathed heavily, craning her neck around to search him out.

He slid his hand in front of her, cradling her sex with it, while still pumping her pussy with his fingers from behind.

"Three more. You can do this." He kissed her shoulder and pressed his body against hers.

"No... oh, no, I can't." She tried to wiggle away, but he had a good grip on her.

His thumb brushed over her clit. Pushing harder,

he rubbed it in a circle. Around and around and around. Her breath came faster, her eyes clenched. She was close already.

"You can and you will. We aren't done here until you do." He wished he had a vibrator handy, it would make it easier, but the manual model would have to do well enough.

Pressing her cheek against the tiles, she turned to face him. He watched her eyes shimmer with frustration and lust. Her lips parted and panting, her body tensing as her orgasm built beneath his fingers.

"Come for me, bad girl," he whispered into her ear, brushing his chin across her shoulder and rubbing her clit faster.

She came unglued. Her eyes clenched shut and her head nearly knocked into his as she cried out toward the ceiling, her orgasm ripping through her. The walls of her pussy clamped down on his fingers as he slowed his strokes, easing her down from her release.

"Trevor." His name escaped her lips on a heavy breath and she pressed her face back into the tile. "No more." She was begging, but he wasn't listening.

"Just two more." He released her body and went about quickly shedding his own clothes. His jeans dragged water out of the tub onto the floor as he dumped them there in a soupy pile.

"I can't. I just can't." Her fingers curled into fists,

but he wouldn't be deterred. She would, and she'd be wonderful.

"Come here." He eased her to sit on the edge of the tub in the corner where it was more stable for her to lean back into the wall. She didn't protest as he positioned her, draping one leg over the faucet and the other over his shoulder, completely exposing her pussy to his view. Even being a little pink from all of the attention, her clit peeked out swollen and aroused.

He moved down to his knees, the water level grazing his hard cock as he moved into position. He kissed the inside of her knee, then trailed down her thigh until his mouth hovered over her pussy.

"It's too sensitive." She tried to cover herself, but after one glare from him, she put her hands on her thighs.

"You tried to take what wasn't yours when you tried to steal my car, Addison." The water sloshed around him as he moved to his knees, bringing his face directly in front of hers. "These orgasms don't belong to you, Addison. They're mine, and I want them." He didn't care if he made any sense at the moment. He only wanted her to learn to obey him, to surrender without hesitation or question.

Her eyes searched him for a long moment. He waited for her objection, more attempts to get out of what he planned, but she remained silent. A plea settled in her eyes for him, but he wasn't giving into that.

"Who owns this?" He placed a hand over her pussy, slipping one finger into her still tight and still soaked passage. "Who owns this pussy, sweet-cheeks?"

She licked her lips before answering, "You do."

"Damn right." Opening his hand, he exposed her clit to his mouth and captured it between his lips. She sucked in air, and squirmed her hips beneath his mouth. He had her effectively trapped in the corner; she wouldn't be going anywhere.

Fuck, she tasted good. Like nectar seeping straight from the heavens. Curling his tongue, he flicked her swollen clit, smiling into her pussy as she yelped. Sensitive little nub. He flicked it again and again, pumping his fingers in and out of her.

Her thigh muscles tensed on either side of him, and one hand came to rest on his head.

"Too much!" she cried, trying to wiggle away and push him off, but his free hand reached up and gave her breast a harsh slap.

"Stay still, and give me another one," he muttered into her pussy. Pumping harder, he sucked on her clit.

The dam opened, and she screamed out into the room again as another orgasm caught her off guard. Her muscles spasmed and pulsed around his fingers, but he didn't give her any reprieve.

He pushed back from her, pulling her legs down

and flipping her over on her stomach, pressing her over the edge of the tub so her ass was to him.

With one quick thrust, he buried himself inside of her, wrapping his arm around her body until he found that little button of hers. Still engorged, and probably too tender for her liking, he flicked it, and rubbed it.

"Oh, fuck!" she yelled out into the room. "Trevor! No... too... much..." She gulped in air between words, trying to climb away from him but he was pounding her from behind, his hand digging into her waist as he rode her.

"One more, give me one more."

"I can't!" she yelled out but after a few more thrusts and more attention from his skilled hands, another orgasm hit her. "Oh, god!" It wasn't the cry of a woman finding ecstasy, but a woman emptied of lust and arousal. A woman enduring an overload of sensory and titillating pleasure.

He found his own orgasm, pumping into her with a hard thrust and growling out his release. When he caught his breath, he slid down into the tub, pulling her with him. Resting against the wall, he cradled her in front of him, pushing her head against his chest and rubbing his hands up and down her arms.

Her breathing calmed, and she lay soft in his arms. "How can you be so fucking perfect?" he asked softly.

She snuggled up against him, splashing the water with her movement.

"I think you broke my clit," she whispered in return.

He snorted when he laughed.

Addison sat on the edge of the bed watching him sleep. The man had snorted when he'd laughed, and it had been the most heartwarming snort she'd ever heard.

After the declaration of her broken anatomy, he'd laughed and hugged her tightly to him. She didn't comment on the little sound, instead she'd snuggled into him and enjoyed the feel of his chest rumbling with pleasure beneath her.

An odd feeling to have toward the man who'd strapped her, paddled her, and forced heart-wrenching orgasms from her already wrung-out body, yet she felt at peace, safe in his arms. That he held her tightly and kissed her cheek only intensified a bond she knew was already forming.

A bond that both excited and terrified her. They couldn't have anything other than the next few days together. Once Steven's murder was solved, and the men responsible were taken into custody, Trevor would trek off back to his part of the city and leave her in hers.

And what part was there for her anymore? Her father would be furious.

"Hey, you okay?" he asked, his voice scratchy from sleep. They'd gone to bed early the night before. Her bath time had worn them both out.

"Yeah. I'm fine." She put on a smile. "You sleep okay?" He hadn't let her go back to her own room. Another rule, she was to sleep with him unless otherwise notified. It wasn't a hard rule to accept by any means.

Swiping his hand across his face, he pushed himself up with his free hand and leaned back against the headboard. The man looked even more dangerous in the morning with his sculpted chest and bed-worn hair tousled around. The stubble on his chin didn't do anything to make him less appealing either.

"You looked awfully deep in thought to be fine." He moved his hand to rest on her knee, squeezing it until she looked at him directly.

"I'm fine. Really." Breakfast before deep conversations, her new motto. "Are you hungry? I think I saw some frozen waffles in the freezer."

He kept looking at her in silence. Like he wasn't sure if he should push for more out of her or not.

She let her lips curl into a grin as she hopped off the bed. "C'mon. I make a mean frozen waffle. Besides you did all the cooking yesterday."

"Okay. Let me just wash up and I'll be down. Don't go outside."

She rolled her eyes out of habit. "I think we've covered that rule pretty diligently." Her cheeks heated. Her ass was still tender, just like almost everything from the waist down thanks to his lessons. Though she couldn't say she hated it. She definitely hated being punished, he wasn't fun and easy when he was in his disciplinarian mode, but she didn't hate the after-effects.

"Just making sure." He gave her a wink and lay back against the headboard, half closing his eyes. "Unless you want to go another round, you should get those waffles in the toaster." As much as another round with him would undoubtedly prove to be ungodly and delicious, her clit was still sensitive from his attention in the tub.

Addison found some coffee to go along with the waffles, and even scored a pint of fresh strawberries. She just finished plating up the food when Trevor walked into the kitchen, grinning at her like some sort of horny teenager.

"Damn, maybe instead of keeping you naked, I'll just keep you in an apron." He pointed at her attire, or lack thereof. She only had one more clean shirt in her bag and hadn't wanted to risk getting syrup on it. Even with basic toaster strudel she managed to get jelly in places it shouldn't be. Jeans and an apron were good enough for the breakfast table, she had figured.

"Ha ha. Funny." She carried the plates to the kitchen island where he already sat on a stool.

"Where'd you find the strawberries?"

"Fridge. Does your friend come up here a lot?"

Trevor lifted one shoulder before stuffing a forkful of waffle into his mouth. "If there's fresh strawberries, he was planning on making a trip up here soon. He owns a bar in the city, and it doesn't take as much time away as it used to."

"I thought he was a cop like you."

"Ex-cop. Ex-marine, too." He lifted his fork and pointed at her plate. "Eat up before it gets cold."

"Did you work with him? Is that how you know him?" She stabbed a piece of waffle and swirled it around the puddle of syrup she poured.

"No, he worked with my brother, uh—you sure you have enough syrup there?"

She didn't miss the undertone of humor in his voice and when she looked up at him, his grin caught her off guard. Completely void of all the seriousness he'd been exuding since they'd met. She was struck with the impression that he really was a laid-back guy, not typically wound as tight as he'd been.

"I like syrup." She smiled back at him. She mopped up more onto the waffle and picked it up off the plate; holding it over her opened mouth, she let the syrup drip off the toasted pastry and into her mouth. Once the sticky goodness had all been poured off, she used her teeth to scrape it off the fork before giving him another sultry smirk.

His lips thinned in a line, and his eyes darkened. "I'm never taking you to eat at a restaurant if you're going to eat your breakfast like that."

She nearly choked on the waffle with her laugh. Just as a witty comeback sprang to mind, a deafening buzzer went off overhead. She dropped her fork to cover her ears while trying to find the source of the obnoxious sound.

"Fuck." He pushed off from the table. "Go to the playroom, Addison. Go now and lock the door." He pointed down the hall.

She didn't want to go there, but when she started to form an argument, his eyes narrowed at her. It wasn't the time for arguing. She nodded and padded down the hall. He went with her, punched the key code in, told her what it was, and waited for her to shut and lock the door from the inside.

With the door closed she couldn't see or hear anything going on outside the room. Her stomach fluttered. She trusted him. She had no other choice at the moment. Whatever was going on out there, he was handling it.

When she heard the familiar beeps of the keypad being used on the outside, she bit off a nail she'd been chewing. She moved to the nearest wall, flattening herself against it.

The door opened, and Trevor stepped in, looking around and visibly relaxing when he found her pressed against the wall.

"What was it?" she asked before he had a chance to say anything.

"We have to go." He tossed her last clean t-shirt at her.

She quickly replaced the apron with real clothing. He held out his hand to her.

She looked at his hand and swallowed. She could badger him for answers and delay them, or she could trust him and follow his lead. Her hand slipped into his, and his fingers curled around it.

"Where are we going?"

"Out of here. The Stephanos brothers found us; that stupid cell of yours. The surveillance picked them up a few miles down the hill, we have about ten minutes before they get up here. Forget your bag, we just have to go."

"We're just going to leave? I thought you said this place was safe."

"It is safe. It will be even safer if we aren't in it when they get here. Now let's go." He pulled her down the hall, through the kitchen to the front door. He gave her enough time to slip on her shoes, but then flung open the front doors and led her down to his car.

"I don't understand," she said again once inside his car.

"Blake has a hunting shelter." The car fired up and he threw it into gear, getting them turned around and down the driveway. "We'll stay there until they leave."

She fastened her seatbelt as he took a turn down a dirt road.

"What if they don't leave?"

He didn't answer.

14

They'd found them a hell of a lot faster than Trevor thought they would. The secluded cabin gave them some cover from the outside world, enough that it should have covered them even when she had used her tracked cell phone. Unless they had another way of tracking her down.

"Did you tell your friend where you were?" Trevor drove his car off the dirt road and through dead leaves and fallen branches, wishing for the first time that he was driving something other than his sedan.

"No. I didn't say who I was with or where we were." She held onto the door handle as the car jostled through the rough terrain until he pulled to a stop.

He parked behind the largest brush he could find and cut the engine.

"Trevor, I didn't." She laid her hand on his arm.

"I know." He nodded and craned his neck to peer out the back window. "This will have to do." He popped his door open and began looking for any large branches he could use to cover the car. A little more camouflage wouldn't hurt.

"How'd they find us? You broke my phone." She began picking up what she could find near her and bringing the branches over to him.

"Yeah, but the signals were still out there. They probably used the signals from the towers nearby. Blake owns most of this land up here, there aren't other houses around." He took the bundle of dirty branches from her arms and laid them over the trunk of the car, hoping it shielded it enough from the road to be missed. "But we're far enough out—" He paused. "Do you have another phone? An iPad, anything like that with your stuff?"

"Just my iPod Touch."

"I didn't see it in your bag, where was it? You don't still have it on you, do you?" Any electronic device, especially Apple devices could be used to track her. They only needed to use the device location service to do it.

"No, it was tucked in a pocket in the bag. But I didn't even turn it on."

Taking a deep breath, he shook his head. "It doesn't need to be turned on if the settings are done right. They were probably using an app designed to find the device even when it's not on."

He gripped her hand and started walking further into the woods.

Her hand trembled beneath his as they walked, stepping over fallen trees, crunching dead foliage on the ground. She didn't have a jacket with her, and she'd only been wearing a t-shirt in the house. Blake would have firewood at the hunting shelter, but it would be a risk to start a fire.

When they came upon the shelter, he let go of her hand and instantly regretted the loss. Blake used to use the shelter for actual hunting, but recently he'd talked about converting it into an outdoor play space. Trevor hadn't asked if he'd finished it or not, but he was about to find out.

"Stay here." He pointed to the porch. "I'm just going to look around."

She stepped up onto the wooden porch and leaned against the door, folding her arms over her chest but not speaking her mind. She didn't need to. She was tired and starting to get annoyed at being bossed around so much. But it was the fear he saw in her eyes that spoke loudest to him. "What do you say when I tell you to do something, Addison?"

"What?"

"When I give you an order, an instruction. What should you say to acknowledge you heard me?" He planted his feet and stared directly up at her from the bottom of the steps.

"You want to discuss etiquette now?" She dropped her arms to her sides and focused on him.

"Answer me, Addison."

She huffed and looked away from him, off into the distance behind him, past where they'd come from and into the trees. There were dangerous men out there, waiting to find her and take her back to Chicago. Men who didn't care about her desires, or her safety. Men who only cared about the damage she could inflict with the information she had. Yes, he wanted to talk about etiquette with her, because that's all the control she had at that moment.

When she brought her gaze back to his, the fear had subsided. "Yes, Sir."

Two words that held more weight at that moment than any other two she could have uttered. "Good. I'll be right back."

He jogged behind the cabin, looking for the place Blake stashed the spare key. Hopefully, he hadn't moved it when he renovated the place. Trevor found the rock in the same place as he remembered it, and turned it over. A few swipes of dirt later he found the little hide-a-key and made his way back to the front to get Addison inside where she could warm up.

The porch was empty. He looked around. He hadn't heard footsteps, or talking or a scream. Just as he was going to call out for her, the door swung open and Addison stood with a blanket wrapped around her shoulders, smiling.

"It was unlocked."

He let out a breath and shook his head. "Where were you supposed to stay, sweet-cheeks?" He climbed the four steps in two strides and met her at the entrance.

"It was cold." She tightened her grip on the blanket. It was cold. The crisp fall air bit at her cheeks, leaving them tinted pink.

"Doesn't really matter, does it?"

"Sorry." Her eyes lowered from his, and if he hadn't been watching her expression so intently he might have missed the small curve to her lips.

"Get inside." He stepped forward, effectively backing her into the cabin.

The shelter was more than just a hunting cabin. Blake had remodeled it to fit his own personal needs all right. Trevor shut the door and leaned against and watched her as she went to the bed and sat on the edge.

"Your friend has a lot of toys." She eyed the wall Trevor was leaning against. He pushed off and took a look, letting a chuckle escape.

"I don't think these are his." He pointed to the male chastity devices. "Well, I guess they could be, but it doesn't seem like his thing."

"Who has a playroom in the middle of the woods like this?" she asked, scooting further on the bed.

Beside the small toy chest, the room consisted of a bed, a fireplace, a small kitchenette, and enough rings built into the walls to keep half a football team chained up.

"There are some things about Blake that I don't know, and I'm not asking." He picked up an extra-large ball gag that hung on the peg board and shook his head. That ball was not meant for a female mouth.

"Do you think they'll find us here?"

"I think you should lie back and rest while I make a few more calls and figure a way out of this mess." He plucked his phone from his back pocket and headed back to the door. "I mean it, Addison. Lie back and rest."

"You're always telling me to rest. I don't want rest, I want to help." She threw off the blanket and shoved herself off the bed.

"Fine. You can get the fire started." He pointed to the stack of wood sitting beside the fireplace. "I'm sure you can figure it out." And with that he went outside and dialed up Blake.

GET THE FIRE STARTED! Did he think she was a Girl Scout? Addison flung the fleece blanket onto the bed and stalked to the fireplace. She'd seen Steven build a fire in his condo more than once, but she'd never paid much attention to how he did it. In her defense, she was usually either tied up or kneeling somewhere close by waiting for him.

Addison picked up a thick piece of wood and placed it on top of the old, singed piece sitting in the fireplace. She sat back on her heels and watched it, blowing a strand of hair from her face. Looking around, she got an idea for what needed doing and started to splinter a small piece of wood and make a pile.

By the time the door opened again and Trevor stepped back in, allowing some of the chilled air to enter with him, she was kneeling in front of the beginnings of a fire. The little flame caught the chipped pieces and spread until the log itself finally caught.

She looked over her shoulder at him with a triumphant smile, expecting to see pleasant surprise. She was met with an icy stare and firmly set jaw.

"What's wrong?" She shot to her feet and faced him.

His expression softened, but it looked forced. He was hiding something, protecting her from something.

"Nothing." He nodded at the fire. "You got it going, I see."

"Something's wrong. You went out looking mildly annoyed, and came back in looking ready to kill. And since I stayed here, I know it's not me. So, what happened on that call?"

He sighed, dragging his fingers through his hair. "We'll talk about it later. Right now, let's get you warmed up. We aren't staying here for much longer, but it's gotten colder outside." He bolted the door and walked past her to the fire. "You did a good job here."

"Why can't you just tell me now?" She went to the bed and sat on the edge. The shelter had no real room to roam around in. Either she sat on the bed, or the rocking chair near the fire.

"I found out who uses this place." Another topic change, but at least it was mildly interesting.

"Oh, really?"

"Yeah. Turns out, Blake let his brother remodel it. It's his. Blake hasn't even been up here to see it." Trevor picked up the poker and started to move the logs around the fire, the flames cascading an orange hue over his features, his stubble-covered stern jaw.

"So the ball gag, chastity stuff is his?" She hadn't had time to look through the little treasure chest of toys, but she'd seen what Trevor had noticed.

"Or his boyfriends, not sure. I don't know much about his brother. He's younger."

"Is he cute?" She enjoyed the possessiveness that flashed through his eyes with her tease.

"No. And he's not your type either." He poked the wood again and put the poker back in its holder.

"And how do you know what my type is?" She couldn't help pushing him when he looked at her with such dominance.

He took three slow steps to the bed and leaned over her, trapping her between his hands as he placed them on the bed. The fresh forest scent still lingered on him.

"Should I show you what your type is? Do you need a reminder of who you belong to?" His words were harsh, but his tone sultry. He pressed his lips to hers briefly before running his tongue over them and resting his forehead against hers. "I can show you if you need."

"I-uh." Her mind wasn't catching up to the conversation.

"Better yet. You show me, sweet-cheeks. Get naked and get on your knees." He shoved off the bed and stepped aside to give her room.

She'd been teasing him, but now he looked hell bent on paying her back. She slid off the bed, standing to the side of him, and holding the hem of her t-shirt. She didn't have any other clothes with her now, and he looked ready to tear it off if she didn't get moving.

"Wait." He put a hand in the air. "Get on your knees, then take off your shirt. I don't need your pants off to fuck your mouth." He unbuckled his belt; the jangle of the metal acted like a tool in one of Pavlov's experiments.

Addison moved to her knees before him, keeping her eyes on his while she positioned herself. When she was where he wanted, he stepped up to her, grabbing a fistful of her hair and pulling her head back.

"Never mind the shirt, I just want your fucking mouth." He unbuttoned and unzipped his pants with one hand, and pulled out his thick, hard cock, letting it bob in front of her mouth. "So now, show me who you belong to." He didn't release her hair, but instead used it to maneuver her toward his cock. Her hunger took over and she opened her mouth, feeling the silky-smooth skin of his cock slide over her tongue as he thrust into her mouth.

He hit the back of her throat, and she coughed, placing her hands on his thighs she tried to push away, but he gripped her hair tighter.

"No, you handle it," he ordered and pulled her back to let her gulp in a breath. Once she had her air, he shoved back into her mouth.

Her lips stretched around his cock, her tongue lapped at his head as it passed through. She relaxed her throat as best she could, and tried to breathe through her nose, as he continued to fuck her mouth.

It was a rough fucking, but she wasn't thinking about her discomfort as much as she was concerned with making him happy, and feeling his cum drip into her throat.

Both of his hands were in her hair while his hips

thrust forward toward her. She held still, giving him the control over both the intensity and depth of his strokes. The head of his cock hit the back of her throat hard and she gagged, but he didn't stop, he didn't relent. He owned her mouth at that moment. Hell, he owned every inch of her, and knowing that, feeling that possession as deeply as she felt it right then gave her the will to give over to him.

"Fuck." The word came out as an angry growl, but it was beyond that. He was close, and he wasn't going to stop until he got what he wanted. With no preamble, he pulled her off his cock and bent over to get in her face.

His hand swiped the drool from her chin and wiped it on her shirt. "Do you want to come for me, sweet-cheeks?"

She swallowed, looking up into his dark eyes, feeling the tight pull on her hair and her own saliva drying on her mouth, she could only come up with one answer. "Yes, Sir."

"Then stick your hand down your pants. Make us both come."

"Yes, Sir." She slid her hand into her jeans, quickly finding her slick, swollen nub and exhaling loudly with the pleasure of her own touch.

"There you go, rub that fucking clit while I fuck your mouth. Come when you're ready, but you better come before me, because when I unload, we're done here."

She nearly went cross-eyed with his words. He wasn't just showing her who she belonged to, he was showing her how much of her he owned.

"Yes, S—" Her words were cut off with his cock being thrust back into her mouth. Her eyes watered at the fierceness of his thrusts, but her clit ached for more as she flicked it with her fingertips. She arched her hips into her own hand, fingering her sensitive bud while sucking hard on his cock.

He kept one hand in her hair, while the other went lower, grabbing her breast through her shirt. It was all she needed. She screamed around his cock as her orgasm rocked her.

Taking advantage, he thrust into her mouth. As the waves of her own release shook her core, she heard his cry of pleasure, and felt the hot streams of his cum spurt out into her mouth. He pulled back, letting it cover her tongue and shoot down her throat. Pleasure unlike she'd ever known tore through her. Her sex throbbed from the lingering orgasm, and the rest of her tingled from knowing she'd taken him exactly how he wanted.

"Swallow." He pulled out of her mouth, and covered it with his hand until she swallowed several times. "Good girl." He kissed her forehead, wiped her lips with his hand, and stood at his full height.

She knelt with her head down, gasping for air, and trying to make sense of the cloud swirling around her mind. He'd barely touched her, yet she found such a deep fulfillment in the act of servicing him. Even if she hadn't orgasmed, she would have felt the same way, because it was him.

He crouched down, cupping her chin in his hands and pulling it up until she looked at his face. No more irritation or jealousy, just Trevor checking to make sure she was okay. She almost smiled at the tenderness. Such a contrast to how roughly he'd just been treating her.

"There's a sink over there if you want to get cleaned up before we—" The ground shook beneath her knees, and a thunderous explosion drowned out all sound around her.

She fell to her side, hitting her head on the wood flooring. She saw Trevor's boots as they ran to the door, felt the cold air from outside hit her face as he flung open the door, but still couldn't hear him. He came rushing back in, his hands working on his belt and yelling something.

Sounds came back but they weren't forming words.

"Addison!" He gripped her arms and yanked her up to her feet. "We—go. Have—go!" She nodded, uncertain about what happened but knowing she needed to be with him. He would keep her safe.

"The fire!" she yelled, pointing back at the shelter as he all but carried her down the stairs.

"Don't worry about that." She tried to keep up with him, but she stumbled. He caught her and helped her the rest of the way to the car. He opened the car door, waving her in, but she wasn't watching him anymore. She was watching the black smoke billowing up over the trees.

"The house," she whispered before he shoved her into the car.

15

How the hell was he going to tell Blake his house blew up?

Trevor sighed again, and looked over at the sleeping woman beside him. She'd been in complete shock at first, not understanding what he was saying and making no sense with her replies. After an hour on the road, she'd finally fallen asleep and stopped badgering him for answers.

He had more of those than he wanted to at the moment, and wasn't sure in what order to give them to her. Blake and his buddies had come through. They'd gotten him everything he needed, and tracked down the suspicion he had, proving him right.

He didn't want to be right. For the first time, he wanted to be dead wrong. Because being right meant she was probably going to get hurt. And he wasn't equipped to let that happen. He needed a little more time.

Using her at the hunter's shelter had been wrong. Knowing what he knew, he shouldn't have done it. But she'd teased him, tried to provoke him with all that talk about other men and her type of man. He knew her type of man. Him. He was her type. The man she needed even if she wasn't sure if it was what she wanted.

But Blake had told him what he suspected, and he shouldn't have done it. He should have left it alone and ignored her little jibe. Instead he'd acted like an asshole and taken advantage.

But she complied so easily, so completely, as though obeying him, submitting to his will at that moment was the only thing that mattered to her.

He shook his head. He had to stop thinking that way. She was a job, a woman who needed protecting from the men that hunted her. Nothing else.

She shifted in her seat, lifting her hands over her head and stretching. Her breasts pushed against her shirt, but he forced himself to look away.

"Where are we?" she asked, settling back in her seat.

"Uh, Northern Wisconsin."

"Wisconsin? How long was I asleep?" She leaned over the console to see the clock. "Shit. I slept that long?"

He chuckled. "Yeah, you needed it." He did, too, but even if he pulled over for a few minutes, he wouldn't be able to.

They'd spent the night in a rundown motel in some backwoods town after fleeing Blake's hunting shelter. Trevor had put enough miles between them and the house, so he took the night to get in touch with Blake and a few more of the guys who were helping him on the case. Files were sent back and forth, and the little doubt he was holding onto had been vanquished.

Addison had slept, but fitfully so. After he'd made her get a few hours of sleep, he'd put them back in his car and started driving north. She'd fallen into a deep sleep easily after they'd stopped for a breakfast, just north of the Illinois border.

"Why are we going north? Do you have another friend with a kinky vacation home?" The levity in her voice sounded forced.

"No." He left it at that. It wasn't time for the big discussion, but he knew it had to happen and soon. They were about to cross the border and then it would be no time at all.

"Are we stopping soon? I'm hungry and could use a shower." She twisted underneath her seatbelt and rested her back against the door.

He glanced over at her. "What are you doing? Sit forward. What if the door flies open?"

"What?" She laughed. "The door isn't going to just open on its own. You have to unlock it and open it."

"Addison. Now. Face forward. I'm not asking you."

She sighed but did as he told her, propping her feet on the dash. "So, why missing persons?" she asked, reclining her seat more.

"I wasn't always in missing persons. I worked homicide for a few years." His hands tightened around the steering wheel.

"Why'd you switch? I mean, was it that bad? Homicide unit in Chicago has to be brutal."

She had that pegged pretty well.

"It wasn't the cases. It was the people." He let out a long breath. "Same problem you have with your dad is the same shit I ran into time and again. Start building a case, get close to solving it and then I'd hit a wall. A well-placed wall built by some bureaucrat or politician or anyone else with enough money to fund the block, and the case would go cold."

"Like with Steven's case. The police never got anywhere. My father saw to that."

He glanced over at her, a pain twisting in his chest. He needed to get off that topic.

"Yeah, like that."

"So, you just switched?"

"No. I was reassigned." He flicked on the headlights as they headed over the border. "I had a partner, Miguel. Got too close to something he shouldn't have and ended up dead. When I tried to track down the guys involved, I found almost a whole squad sitting in some pretty deep pockets. Those dirty fuckers turned their backs on Miguel's murder; hell, they probably were involved, but I never got the chance to find out. I was reassigned before I could even start working on getting real evidence. Anything I had discovered disappeared."

His knuckles started to hurt, so he eased up on his grip. The old rage started to build again in his chest. So many cover-ups, so many dirty-ass cops, and he was the one who got booted from homicide.

"Is that why you agreed to help me? Because of all the shit my dad did?"

He looked over at her, at the braid she was busying her hands with, the large eyes she had focused on him.

"At first, I suppose taking down a corrupt ass like your father and the Stephanos family interested me. But now—" He reached over and flicked her hands away from the braid. "Now, I just want to make sure you're safe. You deserve to have everything you ever wanted in life, and no one is going to get in your fucking way."

He snagged the wheel and turned off the highway, taking the exit. One more night, and then he'd face the consequences.

THE MOTEL TREVOR checked them into faced the highway. A car blared its horn, distracting Addison from the sitcom playing on the television. She ran her fingers through her still wet hair, and abandoned the rerun. The water from Trevor's shower stopped, but she barely noticed.

They'd crossed the border. They were in Minnesota. Why would he bring them to Minnesota? She stared between the blades of the blinds out into the darkness of the parking. The only light she could make out came from the highway, where only a few cars drove by.

"Hey? You okay?" Trevor's concerned voice pulled her attention back to the room. She readjusted the towel she had tucked around her body.

"Yeah. Just looking outside. Good shower?" she asked, letting go of the blinds and padding back to the bed.

One towel was wrapped around his waist, giving her a proper view of his hard body, while he used the hand towel to dry his hair.

He stopped and grinned. "Someone used all the hot water, so I had to be quick."

She laughed. "You told me to go first."

"I didn't say to take half an hour. What were you doing in there anyway?"

She'd been wondering what was coming up next for them. Worrying about going back to Chicago and saying goodbye to him. Never seeing him again. The idea tore at her, and she'd been crying. Not wanting for him to see her in such a mess, she'd washed her face a few more times before facing him.

"Enjoying the heat," she lied and lay back against the pillows. "Are you going to tell me where we're going? What are we doing up north? I thought the idea was to get me back home, but you know, safely."

He tossed the hand towel on to the dresser and pulled the towel off his waist.

Eying him, she smiled. "It wasn't that cold of a shower I see." She scooted over toward him when he climbed on the bed, and effectively trapped her between his arms.

He leaned down, brushing his mouth across hers. "You've been a good girl today."

"It was pretty easy." She leaned into the mattress and reached up to touch his face. "I did sleep most of it away. In fact, I don't think I'll be able to sleep at all now." She ran her fingers over his chapped lips, watching his lips as she did so. The man had such kissable lips, and strong arms to hold her. How was she going to lose him and be okay? Losing Steven had been hard, so agonizingly hard, but she found some solace in that he was in a better place, gone from the pains of the earth. Trevor would be out there still. Saving the lost, protecting the weak, and hunting down those that would threaten them. And when he wasn't doing those things, he'd be in the arms of some woman, another submissive who would feel the strength of his dominance, the power of his love.

"I think I can help with that. Roll over." He pushed himself up, jostling the bed as he moved and patted her hip. "And get rid of that towel."

Not willing to ruin his good mood, she obeyed instantly and tossed the damp towel onto a nearby chair. She rolled onto her stomach and moved the pillows to rest on. The bed dipped again when he moved, straddling her thighs. Warm hands ran over her bare ass and she stiffened in reaction.

He laughed. "Relax, I'm not going to punish you for being a good girl. I'm going to reward you." Both of his hands began to rub her backside, rubbing all the way up toward her back.

"A massage?" she asked, peeking over her shoulder at him.

He nodded. "For now." His fingers delved deep into her tissues, relaxing even the tightest spots until she was a limp mess.

"Dear god, you are good at this," she muttered into the pillow.

"Roll back over." He didn't wait for her to obey this time, he simply grabbed her hips and flipped her onto her back. She pushed up to her elbows to give him a glare, but his determined eyes met hers. His tongue slipped out of his mouth and licked his thick lips as he lowered himself on the bed; lying between her thighs, he pushed them wide apart.

"You keep your legs open like this." She'd never been so spread open before. "I want to see your pussy, play with it, kiss it, and lick it. If you close your legs, or even move them, I'll spank your pussy. It's not fun, I promise you. This little clit of yours—" Using the tip of his finger, he toyed with the nub in question. "It's sensitive."

The overuse of her clit the morning before had seen to that. Just the little pressure he put on it with his finger was enough to make her wince.

"I won't move," she promised.

His smile morphed into the dangerous grin she'd come to both fear and crave.

"I'm kind of hoping you do." He winked and leaned further down, blowing a soft breeze over her exposed sex. Her body already wanted him and he'd barely touched her.

His strong fingers dug into her thighs as he swirled his tongue around her clit, holding the hood of her pussy out of the way with his free hand. She arched her back and grabbed at the bedding beneath her, but fought the urge to snap her legs closed.

"Ah, such a good girl for me tonight," he whispered into her pussy. His tongue lashed out, licking her from her eager entrance to her swollen and wanting clit.

His firm grip dug into her again as he sucked her

clit into his mouth with a much higher intensity. She gulped in her breath and tried to hold her legs open for him, to allow him to give her the pain that would bring her the pleasure, but when his teeth grazed the oversensitive bundle of nerves, she lost the battle.

"Ah, ah, ah." Trevor shoved her thighs away from the sides of his head, where she'd trapped him. "There was one rule, what was it?" He held her knees apart, spreading her farther than before.

"Not to move my legs," she moaned. He was enjoying himself too much!

"And you did—so what do you think happens now?" He maneuvered himself on the bed until he was on his knees, kneeling before her, his hard cock in full view.

"Now you're going to spank my pussy." She sounded pitiful. She knew it, but didn't care.

"Yes, I am."

"You don't need to sound so cheerful about it." Pouting was beneath her, but again she didn't care.

"Of course I do. Do you know why?" He trailed his fingertips along her thigh. "Because I love making you squirm and whine. And then I love sinking myself into that tight pussy of yours. And here's a little secret." He bent over, hovering over her as though he were going to whisper. "I know you love it, too."

She grunted and looked away. Of course she did.

"I think ten will do." And before she could get her

bearing, he twisted to hold one leg behind his back and gripped the other, spreading her far and began to lay the smacks down on her pussy. She yelped and wiggled, the fire quickly igniting, the sting nearly unbearable as he concentrated on her clit. He counted out loud; each stroke, each agonizing, punishing smack to her sex was announced into the room with clarity.

When he was finally finished, her chest heaved from heavy breathing, her leg muscles felt stretched, but she had no time to wallow in the discomfort. He was over her, kissing her. His lips punishing her own with a deep, possessive kiss that left no doubt in her mind who she belonged to—who she wanted to belong to.

"Think you can hold those legs open for me now?"

"Yes, Sir." Her answer came out in a whisper. He remained close, his chest pressed against hers, his hard length pressed against her even more tender pussy.

"I'm going to fuck you now. And you are going to hold your legs open, grab your knees, pull them upward, offer that pussy to me." Such crude words softened when he spoke them. He knew exactly what to say and how to say it in order to speak to her heart.

"Yes, Sir." She reached down, hooked her hands behind her knees and pulled them back.

He shifted, pressing the head of his cock to her

entrance. "So fucking wet." He smiled down at her and slowly began to enter her. She waited for the thrust, the hard push into her body, but it never came. He inched his way into her, filling her, stretching her until he was buried inside of her.

She wiggled beneath, seeking more contact, but wanting the pressure to lessen at the same time.

His biceps flexed as he held his position, staring down at her. He looked downright giddy at her discomfort, her urgency.

"Who do you think decides how you get fucked?"

How the hell was he thinking coherently enough to ask such a question?

"You do, Sir," she managed to answer while still wriggling to get him moving. Feeling his cock fill her wasn't enough, she needed him to push, to take her in the most primal of ways. She didn't want soft and tender, she wanted a hard claiming.

Remaining still, he lowered himself until his nose touched hers. "That's right, sweet-cheeks."

"Please, Sir," she whispered, arching herself up to meet him. His lips curled into a wide smile, pulling his cock back and nearly completely out of her. In one powerful thrust he was back inside of her, giving her exactly what her body wanted. His complete ownership.

He groaned against her shoulder, kissing and nipping at the tender skin as he thrust again and again into her. She met each stroke, lifting her hips to meet his, charging after the ending only he could give her.

Each powerful thrust pushed her closer, but he kept her at bay, not touching her clit. The place that would send her spiraling over the edge.

"Please, Sir. Please, Trevor." She pulled her legs back toward her more, spreading herself even wider for him.

He made an animalist sound and bit down hard on his bottom lip. "Fuck, sweet-cheeks." He brought his mouth to hers. "I'm going to flick that clit of yours, and you're going to come for me. Am I understood?" Like a rabid beast, he growled when she pulled her legs back again. "Addison." The warning came through crystal clear. The only teasing that would take place was from him to her, not the other way around.

"Yes, Sir. I understand."

"Good." He nodded, kissing her. So focused on his mouth, the feel of his tongue sliding past her lips and dancing with her own, she didn't realize his hand had slid between them until his fingers were on her clit, probing and pinching. "Come for me, sweet-cheeks. I want everyone in this hotel to know who owns you, who's fucking you right now."

Her clit was still tender, still sensitive from his punishments, but it didn't register. Nothing mattered except he was taking her, claiming her, and wasn't apologetic for it. He wasn't tenderly stroking her or singing her sonnets. He took her. He brought her to places she didn't think she could go. He pushed her, pulled her, and wound her up until she couldn't control her own body, until she no longer wanted to do anything other than give over to him. Submit completely to him.

It could have been his fingers, or his words, or the deep kiss he began again, she didn't know what caused it, because her mind lost touch with reality. Her body jolted, bucked beneath him, as the waves of the explosion rocked through her. She cried out, at first into his mouth as he kissed her, and then into the room when he broke the kiss and began fucking her even harder.

"Trevor!" she shouted, letting go of her knees and grabbing hold of his shoulders. She didn't care if the people in the next room heard them, she called out to him, not wanting her orgasm to fade away too quickly. His fingers dug into her hips as he pinned her to the mattress, as his own orgasm took over.

One second he was buried inside of her, filling and stretching her, the next he was kissing her. Not the deep, possessive kiss from their coupling, but tender and full of emotion. "You are damn perfect, sweet-cheeks," he whispered against her mouth. "Absolutely perfect."

16

Maybe he was wrong; maybe it wasn't going to turn out the way he now feared. But he wasn't wrong. He rarely was. He could read perfectly well. He hadn't made a mistake.

Trevor watched Addison walk to the restroom of the restaurant where they were having breakfast. Sleeping with her curled up next to him, her leg thrown over his as she slept had been as natural as sleeping naked. He didn't even mind the soft snore she acquired once she'd dove into deep sleep. A soft sound being emitted by the most beautiful creature he'd ever laid his eyes on.

"More coffee?" The waitress hovered a coffee carafe over his nearly empty cup.

"No, thanks." He pushed the mug away from him. "Just the check, please." He looked over at the half-eaten breakfast still sitting on Addison's plate. He needed to tell her, and just be quick about it.

He pulled out his phone again, rereading what Blake sent him. There was no mistake.

"What's so important on your phone today? You've been staring at it all morning. Anything I should know?" Addison slid into her seat at their booth.

After turning off his screen, he placed it face down on the table.

"Yeah." He cleared his throat and fidgeted in his seat. "Actually, we do need to talk about something."

She picked up her toast and nibbled on the corner of it. "Okay then," she prodded after swallowing, and he still hadn't said anything. "What is it?"

"Here's your check." The waitress dropped the handwritten bill on the table on her way to bringing another table's order out to them.

"I'm gonna pay this. Finish your food." He pointed at her plate. "We aren't leaving until all the eggs are gone." He ignored her confused expression as he slid out of the booth. *Coward and an asshole.*

The cashier wasn't a day under ninety-three, which suited him just fine. The elderly woman readjusted her glasses half a dozen times while punching in keys on a register that was clearly as old as she. Once she handed him back his change he thanked her and headed back to Addison. As soon as he told her, they could go.

His phone wasn't on the table when he got back. It was in her hands, and she was reading it, scanning and flipping through.

"What are you doing?" He forced irritation in his voice, but he knew exactly what she was doing.

"Is this true?" She watched him with wide eyes as he sat back down. "All of this stuff, is this true?" She shook his phone at him.

"I was getting ready to tell you. It's why we're here." He reached over and plucked the phone from her. Her cheeks flushed, but not with the innocent arousal he'd grown to love over the past days.

"Getting ready? How long have you known?" She planted her hands on the table, palms down and fingers splayed out. If she was going to pounce at him, she was set and ready.

"Addison. Lower your voice," he commanded, feeling eyes starting to turn their way. "Let me explain."

"I don't think you need to. I think I read everything I need to know." Acid laced her words.

"You shouldn't have picked up my phone." Deflect and deny. Great. Now he was using the very behavior he despised.

"I wanted to see what time it was, and you broke my phone, remember?"

He didn't point out that there was a clock on the wall behind her. She probably hadn't seen it, and regardless, the cat was out of the bag, and looking willing to claw his eyes out.

"Yes, what you read is true. Blake verified it several times before sending it to me."

"Steven." Tears built in her eyes, sparkling in the sun shining through the diner window. "He's alive?"

Trevor nodded. "Yes. He's alive. He lives in this town, actually." He looked out the window, at the few people walking down the street. It wasn't a small town by any means, and the likelihood of Steven walking past them at that moment was pretty small.

"You brought me to him? Do you have his number? Why didn't we call? Why didn't you let me call—why didn't you tell me?" Each question came faster and louder. He clamped his hands over hers tightly, forcing her to focus on him.

"I have my reasons for not telling you right away, and for not trying to call him. We'll go to his house and then see what happens from there."

"What does this mean? I mean, for me, for home? My father told me he was dead. The media posted articles about the accident. His parents! His parents talked to me after the memorial." She tugged her hands free of his and sat back against the seat.

"I think it's more complicated than just a simple lie. Let's let him explain. Okay?"

"How long did you know?"

"Addison."

Dishes rattled when she slammed her hand down on the table. "How. Long."

He sighed. "Since the hunting cabin."

She stared at him with shock filling her features. "I want to go now." She pushed her plate away and scooted out of the booth.

He followed her, tempted to pull her to stop and demand she give him time to explain everything, but she was already at the door. And he needed her to be calm when they got to Steven's house. If what he assumed had happened a year ago, had happened, she was going have one hell of a roller-coaster ride of emotions.

"Well, that could have gone better," he mumbled to himself as he caught the door before it hit him and followed her out to the car.

As soon as he unlocked the doors, Addison flung hers open and jumped into the car. By the time, he'd gotten himself inside and situated she was worked up into a nice thick lather.

"I know this is a shock, but I need you to try to focus, stay calm. When we get there, you let me talk to him first."

"No." She shook her head, but didn't turn to face him. He suspected daggers might actually shoot out at him if she did, but she didn't understand.

"Yes. That's the deal. I'll take you to him, but you let me talk."

"Why?" The demand came with a heated glare.

"Because you're coming at this emotionally, and I need answers," he said.

"Emotionally? Fuck you!" she said. "For the past year, I've been thinking he's dead! Dead! Do you know what that felt like? No, you don't. I want answers, too. And mine come first."

"Addison, you can stay in the car if it makes it easier for you. I'll go in, talk with him then you can come inside." It seemed to be a good compromise. She could get herself together while he sorted out all the messed-up lies and events that led Steven to living peacefully in Minnesota while he'd left Addison to deal with her asshole of a father on her own.

He needed to see for himself what sort of man could do that. Addison wasn't weak, not by any shred of truth, but she had needed Steven. And now, even if she wouldn't admit it, she needed Trevor.

"I'll go on my own." She reached the door handle, but he managed to get a hold on her and pull her close to him.

Wrapping his arm around her chest, he kept her still against his own. "Listen to me, Addison. The rules haven't changed. I know you have a lot going on in your head right now, but you will focus on me, and you will obey the rules I've given you. I can still spank you before we get there. That's not a problem for me."

Her body settled in his hold.

"Okay. Okay." She nodded and tapped his forearm with her hand. "But, I want to talk to him first." The crackled anguish in her voice nearly undid him.

"Okay, but if you talk to him first, then I have to at least be in the room. I need to see his reactions to know if he's lying or not."

"Fine." She nodded again. "Let me go. Please."

The fight was gone from her voice and her body nearly limp in his arms. He released her, and she surprised him by not trying to flee the car. Instead she strapped herself in and stared out the window. Trevor kept a watchful eye on her as he started up the car and pulled into traffic.

Her hands were already working on a new braid.

STEVEN WAS ALIVE? No. No question. Steven was alive. Period. He'd been alive the whole time. Every moment she'd mourned him, cried for him, and felt as though her heart was being ripped from her chest, he'd been alive and well in Minnesota.

And Trevor. He knew. Had known for almost two days. Her head hurt thinking about it all. In those two days, they'd had sex multiple times. He'd kissed her like no one, not even Steven, had kissed her before. He'd held her while she slept. They'd connected.

Or so she thought.

To him, she was just a fuck toy. A submissive to play with while on a stupid assignment given to him by his boss back in Chicago. And she'd fallen for his act. Had taken him to heart, had let him in her heart.

She groaned and rested her head against the window as he turned down another street. Her heart. She'd completely pushed Steven out and had made room for Trevor. She had trusted him. She had thought he knew her, understood her like no one else could.

"Here it is." Trevor's soft voice sounded more like a jackhammer as he pulled the car up to a curb. She looked up at the house. A Victorian farmhouse. "Remember—"

"I know." She didn't bother looking at him as she pushed the car door open and stepped out. He could stand right next to her, she didn't care. She only wanted to see Steven. To find out what the hell had happened. Why had she put her life on the line making a case for his murder, when it hadn't happened?

She could feel Trevor walking right behind her. Hell, she could sense the tension in his body as she climbed the steps. It mirrored her own, but she wasn't going to lean on him. She was not going to do anything with him ever again.

Taking a deep breath, her finger hovered over the

doorbell. "Steven's alive," she whispered to herself and forced herself to push the button.

A dog barked as the bell rang. A few seconds later a shadowed figure came to the door. A bolt slid from the door. The handle turned.

Trevor placed his hand on her shoulder, but she shook it off.

Finally, the door opened.

"Steven." She breathed out his name, complete shock running through her body. She'd known. Trevor had confirmed it, but to see him standing there. His dark hair parted to the side like she remembered. The clean-cut collared shirts he always wore, perfectly pressed and tucked into his jeans. Everything was exactly as she remembered it.

"Addy?" His green eyes widened in surprise, or fear? He looked over her shoulder at Trevor then back at her. "What are you doing here?"

He hadn't opened the screen door yet to let her in. Didn't he want to touch her, to hold her? But she hadn't reached for it either.

"You're here," she said. She waited for an overwhelming emotion to take hold, but nothing happened.

"Come in." Steven swung the screen door open. "It's cold out here," he muttered as an afterthought, though Addison noticed him checking the street behind her as she walked past him.

She caught a note of his cologne. Nothing had changed.

Once they were inside she walked into the living room to the left of the entrance. Taking in the beauty of the room, the paintings hanging on the walls, the tapestry, and the furniture, she spun around to face him.

"Is this your house? I mean, do you live with someone?"

Steven stood in the doorway, wringing his hands. Gone, it seemed, was the strong dominant man she remembered. In his place stood a frightened shell of the man from her memories.

His eyes darted to Trevor then back to her. "I—well, yes."

"I don't understand."

"Addison." Steven stuffed his hands into his pockets and took a deep breath. "I didn't think... We weren't meant to ever see each other again."

"Obviously, since you are supposed to be dead!" she yelled at him. Never in their relationship had she so much as raised her voice to him. He was her dominant, her leader. Yelling at him had never registered as something she would do. Ironic, since Trevor had the opposite effect on her.

"I know this is surprising—"

"Why? You just left? Let me think you were killed?"

Steven made no move to touch her, though she

doubted his hands would have the soothing effect she remembered. Trevor moved, though; he stood beside her. And angry as she was, sensing him so close kept her from lunging at Steven.

"It's complicated. Your father didn't want you to marry me."

"Yeah. I know. I told him to stay out of it, remember?" Her body tensed with the rage boiling beneath the surface. Taking that stand with her father hadn't been easy for her, but for Steven she would have faced even her father's disappointment.

"He wasn't going to stay out of it, Addy. He—he insisted that I leave, that I break it off and leave. But he knew you wouldn't leave it at that."

"He offered you money," Trevor interjected. "There's a bank transfer of two million right before the car accident took place."

"What?" Addison turned to face Trevor. "The police checked all of that, his bank records, his phone records, during the investigation."

Trevor's eyes softened.

Corruption. More corruption. "There was no real investigation, was there?"

Trevor shook his head, but glanced over at Steven. "No. Not really. From what Blake and his guys found, some smokescreens were thrown up for the reporters, but nothing of substance."

"But the stuff I found. The evidence."

"Bits of information the cops had on file to show they investigated, in case something ever came around. That's why you were able to find so much in your father's office and the Stephanos computers," Trevor explained.

"You went to the Stephanos family for evidence?" Steven's voice darkened. "You investigated them? On your own? Do you know how dangerous that was?"

Addison looked at her ex-fiancé. The same protective glare, but she felt none of the butterflies she'd felt in the past. The connection had dislodged over the year.

He'd taken money to leave her.

"No more dangerous than if I had actually married into that horrible family like my father wanted," she shot at him. "You left me, just left me behind to fight against him alone." She'd fought everything alone since he'd left.

"Addy—"

"Don't." She put a hand up when he finally stepped closer to her. "I think I understand everything. You didn't want to fight my father and his bullies, so he offered you cash to run and you took it. Bought this gorgeous house, got a new girl, and forgot all about me." Tears burned her eyes. Her chest cramped and her nails bit harder into her palms.

"I never forgot. I figured you'd be married by now."

"Married?" She couldn't help but laugh. "You thought that I'd just pick up and move on?"

Steven looked at Trevor. "Didn't you?"

She blinked. Had she? As angry as she was at Trevor at the moment, she had been with him. They'd fucked. They'd kissed. She'd let him punish her.

Trevor stepped in front of her, blocking her view behind his broad back.

"I think you and I need to talk. Addison, why don't you find the kitchen and get something to drink."

She glared at his back. Being sent away like a child who didn't need to hear the adults talking? Fuck. No.

"You know, I think I'd rather wait in the car if it's okay." She tapped his back.

He turned around, looking down at her with more concern in his eyes than she'd ever seen before. Just an act, she reminded herself. Just another ploy to get what he wants. He needed answers from Steven, that's all it was.

"It's cold out there."

"Can I turn the car on for heat?" she asked, putting her hand out.

He glanced at her open palm. "You'll stay in the car? No wandering off? I'll be just a few minutes." He had already put his hand in his pocket for the keys as he asked.

"Of course, Trevor." She lowered her voice. "I'm aware of the consequences."

Trevor looked a little surprised, but not unpleased at her words. He dropped the keys, along with the square remote into her hand. "Okay, then."

"Thanks." She walked around him, passed Steven with a shaky breath, and headed for the front door.

"Addy. Wait." Steven rushed to the door. "I'm sorry. So sorry. Your dad never would have left us alone. And those people he deals with—they never would have let it go either."

"I get my father. He's a selfish old man who has always tried to control me, and letting me move up here with you wasn't something he was willing to do. But, you were supposed to protect me. You swore to always be there for me. But you sold me, too. Just like the rest of his goons." Her voice shook, and she hated that. Hated that she couldn't control the anger inside of her. Everyone had something to win by betraying her.

"I'm sorry."

She didn't respond. Sorry wasn't a big enough word to let him off the hook for what he had done. Opening the door, she didn't bother to look back. He may not have died a year ago, and he may be standing right in front of her at that moment, but as far as her heart was concerned he was buried in her past.

Addison shut the door behind her and jogged down the steps of the porch to Trevor's car.

Steven had played dead to get away from her, and

Trevor had pretended much worse. He had acted like he cared. Really cared about her. He'd let her feel things she didn't think she'd ever feel again, and it was all a lie.

The car started up with no trouble, and with very little sound. She leaned over the passenger side to look into the picture window of the living room. Trevor's back was to the window, and he was gesturing with his hands. She wondered if he'd actually punch Steven. He had looked a bit willing to throw a few fists when they'd walked into the house, and even more so after he'd seen her reaction to Steven's confession.

"No. It was all a lie," she muttered.

Throwing the car into gear, she pulled out of the parking space and into the quiet traffic of the suburban town.

No matter what Trevor was doing with Steven. No matter what Steven would be able to help with now. She didn't care about any of it. She was done. The game was over.

She was going home.

17

Addison wouldn't be able to sit for at least a full week when he got his hands on her. He had had enough trouble keeping his anger in check while Steven answered her questions, then he had to listen to the coward as he answered his own. And the entire time the woman he was protecting, the woman who had turned his world inside out, had been driving off with his car!

Watching Steven crush her and not getting involved had taken more strength than he thought he possessed, but Addison wouldn't have accepted his help. Not at that moment. He'd known Steven had taken money from her father, but he hadn't realized how easy it had been for him to take it and run. Addison hadn't broken down like he feared she might. No, his Addison was made of stronger stuff.

And more stubborn than he thought possible.

Trevor stood at the car rental office waiting for the keys to whatever car they had available. The small office smelt of burnt coffee, and obviously hadn't been renovated since the late seventies.

His phone started to buzz in his pocket, and he whipped it out.

"You want to tell me what the fuck happened to my cabin?"

Blake. "I had some trouble." A black Honda Civic pulled up to the front doors of the office and the young man that had been helping him hopped out dangling the keys in his hand. "I'm still having trouble."

"Trouble? I've been talking to cops all fucking morning. The place was blown up, Trevor. Blown up, like with explosives."

"I'll pay for the damages, but I need—"

"Damages? There's nothing left!"

"Blake!" Trevor ripped the keys from the kid and jumped in the car, jamming the key into the ignition. "She's gone."

"What? What do you mean gone?" Instantly the anger subsided from Blake's voice, replaced with genuine concern.

"She's mad that I didn't tell her right away about Steven, and meeting Steven didn't go so well. She took my car and drove off."

Trevor pulled out of the lot and headed to the highway. She had no money and no clothes; she had to be heading home.

"Why didn't you tell her?"

"I don't know. I thought it was better to wait."

"Better for who?"

Trevor gripped his phone tighter.

"Don't start that shit. I did what I thought was right at the time. That's not the issue. The issue is I haven't talked with her father or the Stephanos family. They are still under the impression she has dirt on them. She's not protected, but she's still being hunted. You get me?"

"They the ones that blew up my cabin?"

"One, that mansion was not a cabin. Two, of course it was them."

"Where do you think she's heading?" Blake asked.

"I'm assuming home. She has about an hour head start on me. I'm gonna try to catch up to her, but if I don't, I need someone at her apartment. Someone to watch out for her until I get there."

"You have an address for me? I'll go over there. The bar's closed today to get some plumbing issues fixed. I'll hang at her place till you get there."

"I was hoping you'd have it. I never expected to find her at her apartment. It was supposed to be a quick trip up to get her and bring her to her father. I left her file at my apartment."

Blake sighed into the phone. "I swear, kid—Fine. I'll trek to your place first, get the address, then I'll head over to hers. You know, between you and your brother it's like I spend all my time fixing your fuck-ups."

"What's wrong with Devin?"

"Nothing a good kick in the ass won't solve. He's fine. He's fixing it. You are the problem in my hands now."

"Just get to her place. She doesn't understand that she's still in danger. Or she does and doesn't care." The second was more likely. He'd seen the hurt in her face at the restaurant when she discovered what he'd kept from her. He'd witnessed it morph into anger, only to see more pain wash that away with Steven's confession.

"I'm on it. When this is over, we'll talk about the cabin."

ADDISON ROLLED OVER IN BED, covering her eyes with her arm to keep the sun from beating into them. Charity needed new blinds. Ones that actually kept the sun out in the mornings.

For a split second, she felt normal. But then the memories all came back to her, hitting her hard. Steven was alive. All that time she'd wasted mourning him. All the danger she put herself in trying to find out the truth about his death. He hadn't even looked ashamed. Just pitiful. Almost fearful when Trevor had stepped forward and taken over the conversation.

Trevor. The familiar bubble formed in her chest when his name crossed her mind. He'd used her. Played with her like some new toy to be cast away when the shine wore off.

Groaning, she pulled her pillow over her face.

"Addison?" Charity's soft voice penetrated through her pillow defenses.

"Go away," she mumbled.

"Addison. You've been in bed for two days." Charity's firm voice was with her; there'd be no getting rid of her now. The door squeaked as it opened completely and she heard Charity's heeled feet step into the room.

"I like being in bed, Charity. Besides. There's no reason to get up."

"Of course there is." The bed jostled as Charity sat down. "You know you can stay here as long as you need. But at some point, you're going to have to call your father and let him know you're back in town."

"Charity. I can't." Addison tossed the pillow away from her face and pulled herself up to sitting. She hadn't explained everything to Charity, she hadn't had the strength.

"Why not?"

"Steven's not dead." She said the words out loud,

and they didn't make her want to hurl something against the wall. "He's living, quite comfortably, in Minnesota with some girl and two millions dollars of my father's money."

"What?" Charity's voice rose a few decibels. Enough for Jackson to come the room.

"Everything okay?"

"Steven's not dead." Charity kept her amazed expression locked with Addison as she said the words.

Addison sighed and closed her eyes for a moment. She told the story, all of it—well, most of it. She told them about the Stephanos family coming for her, how Trevor had saved her, and then took care of her. She explained how he found out about Steven and he took her to him. And she went over everything Steven told her about what happened a year ago.

"Is that whose car you had? Trevor's?"

"Yeah." Addison smiled at that. It had to have pissed him off pretty fierce that she'd stolen his car. Too bad. He deserved it. And more.

"I thought you said he was helping you? You left him?" Jackson didn't sound very sympathetic to her cause.

"He deserved to be left, Jackson."

Jackson pinched the bridge of his nose and sighed. He usually reserved his impatience for Charity, but Addison knew exasperation when she saw it.

"Okay, start at the beginning again. When Trevor picked you up."

"He didn't pick me up, he took me."

"It sounded like he saved you." Charity added and scooted over on the loveseat she was sitting on to make room for Jackson. He shook his head, urged her up, then took her seat, settling her on his lap once he was comfortable.

"From the beginning, Addison," he commanded.

"Doms are just bossy, aren't they, no matter who their sub really is." Addison tried to sounded snarky, but when she saw his eyebrow rise she realized she'd just sounded rude. "I'm sorry, Jackson. I'm just tired, and I don't want to go over this again."

"You've slept for nearly two days." Jackson rested his chin on Charity's shoulder. They looked so at ease with each other. No lies or deception. Almost how it felt to be in Trevor's arms. "Why did he deserve to be left behind?"

Addison closed her eyes and leaned back against the headrest. Because he'd used her like the whore she'd let herself become with him? Or how about because when he knew she'd probably call off their little tryst, he kept her one more night for one last fuck. Or because she'd allowed herself to feel again while in his arms, and it was more than anything she'd felt before.

"Jackson. Didn't you hear me? Steven's alive! Aren't

you concerned about that? I mean, don't you care about that part of this whole story?" she shot back at him.

Jackson lifted his shoulders in a carefree shrug. "I'm not surprised, actually. Addy, I know you loved him, and we never said anything because of that, but he was weak."

Addison looked to Charity for confirmation. The pink tint to her otherwise pale cheeks sealed the deal.

"Weak?"

"Addy, he let you run all over him. The worst punishment you got was a caning, and even that he turned into more of a play session than a real punishment," Charity said.

"What does that have to do with anything? So, he wasn't an overly stern dominant."

"He wasn't an overly anything," Jackson quipped. "He went along with the crowd. Whichever way the wind blew, he went with it. It's no wonder it only took some green to get him to run away."

His words should have pissed her off. Steam should have been ready to blow out her ears. But she just stared at her two closest friends, speechless. Hadn't Trevor mentioned several times that Steven hadn't done her any favors by being so lenient with her?

Jackson patted Charity's hip, signaling for her to get up. Once he was standing again, he took his girlfriend's hand and motioned for the door. "You need to call this Trevor guy to give him his car back. He's a cop, Addison. You can't keep a cop's car."

Charity paused by the door. "I'm wondering, are you more upset that Steven turned out to be complete waste or that you think Trevor never cared about you?"

Addison worked up a decent glare but couldn't bring herself to face Charity with it. Instead she sank back under the covers and pulled them over her head. Even under the thick comforter she could hear Jackson's sigh.

"What's his name, Addison? I'll see if I can track him down to get the car back to him."

Seeing it as a small reprieve to have Jackson deliver the damn car back to Trevor, she offered the information from beneath the blanket. "Trevor Stringer. He's a detective in the missing person's division." She tried to remember the number on his badge. It had been over a week ago since she'd taken a look at it, but it felt lightyears away. "I don't know the precinct."

"Did you say Trevor Stringer?" The comforter peeled back from her grasp and an amused Jackson hovered over her.

"Yeah. So?"

Jackson threw his head back and laughed. Charity looked as puzzled as Addison felt.

"You stole Trevor Stringer's car. Oh. This is. Wow."

He tossed the blanket back over her face. "Come on, Charity. We aren't getting involved in this one."

"Do you know him?" Charity asked, but the door closed before Addison could scramble out from under the blanket to hear the answer.

Just as she popped out of bed, the door reopened and Jackson, still grinning like a loon, peeked his head in. "I have his number. You will not leave this apartment until you call him."

"Why do you think you can boss me around so much? You didn't used to," she shot at him, feeling petulant and childish.

"Because before you were mourning, and I had no idea you were putting yourself into so much danger."

"Jackson, Steven took two million dollars to leave me. Just left me." She sank onto the corner of the bed. The door pushed completely open and Jackson blocked Charity from reentering the room. "Trevor. He —he used me." The tears she'd been keeping at bay started to build in her eyes, but Jackson's features didn't soften.

"Addison, you really should know by now that things aren't always how they appear. I'll get his number for you and leave it on the kitchen table. Charity and I are having lunch with my parents. When we get back, I hope you will have already called him."

"Call him, Addison," Charity called over Jackson's

shoulder.

He rolled his eyes and grabbed the door handle again. "No more sleeping. Shower, dress, and call him."

"Fine," Addison agreed. It would be a cold day in hell before she picked up the phone to call that man.

"Good." He gave a final nod, as though that settled everything and shut the door.

"Do you think she knows she loves him, or is she still fighting it?" Jackson asked Charity just before the door shut.

Love him? Trevor?

No.

Absolutely not.

He'd used her for a fuck toy.

That was all. They played a bit during a stressful time. That was it.

Love?

Just because she missed his touch, and his kisses, and the way he watched her when he didn't think she knew didn't mean she loved him. Sure, the sound of his voice sent shivers through her, and he could set her body aflame with a single look. So what? And it didn't matter either, that when he ran his fingers through her hair and called her his good girl, her insides melted, and she felt as though nothing in the world could touch her. No, that didn't matter.

Except, it totally mattered.

———

18

Trevor stood in the middle of the unfamiliar living room trying to gain control over his anger. It was bad enough the woman had run away from him, stolen his car, but now she was hiding.

Blake had spent nearly two days babysitting an empty apartment, waiting for Addison to show up while Trevor searched the city. Once Trevor arrived at her apartment, he sent him packing. When she walked through that door, they didn't need an audience for what was going to be happening.

Her heart was hurting. Understandable. He had witnessed it, had seen the raw pain flash through her features when she realized Steven had just walked away from her for money. The bastard. The asshole hadn't even given her the kindness of looking remorseful or pretending that the decision had been hard.

Walking away from Addison for any amount of riches or fame seemed ludicrous. So much more was gained with her at his side than any tangible object could give him. How did Steven not see that?

But the answer was pretty clear. Steven never dove into the heart of Addison. He had never touched the center of her submission the way Trevor had. Steven never knew how beautiful her soul really was. Because if he had, rabid lions wouldn't have been able to keep him away from her.

A digital beep sounded from the bedroom—the clock on her nightstand signaling the hour change. Trevor had already inspected the entire apartment, and memorized each room. It wasn't that difficult; for a councilman's daughter she lived quite simply. The apartment wasn't overly large, and the decor didn't reek of wealth.

His first impression of her couldn't have been more wrong. Good thing he was able to get a second and third impression.

"Where the fuck are you?" Trevor grabbed his phone again and texted Blake. Trevor managed to track down a friend's name. His girl liked to keep her private life very private, and Blake was supposed to be finding the address.

His phone rang before he could have finished pounding out the text. An old acquaintance.

"Jackson?" Trevor answered with surprise. He hadn't heard from Jackson Malone in years. They didn't exactly run in the same circles.

"Hey, Trevor. Sorry to call so out of the blue." Hesitation weighed Jackson's voice down.

"No, that's fine. Everything okay?" Trevor went to the front window, peering through the blinds, checking for anyone or anything that looked out of place.

"I think I have who you're looking for."

Trevor's ears peaked. "Addison? You know her?"

Jackson's chuckle wasn't well received, but Trevor managed to keep his irritation at bay.

"She's friends with my fiancée. I've known her for years. I'm guessing you're wanting your car back?"

Trevor groaned. "I'm wanting more than my car back."

"I figured as much. She's hiding out at my place. I told her to call you, but I know Addy, and if she's not in the mind to do something, she's not going to do it. Well, without the proper motivation anyway." Car horns blared in the background.

"You left her alone? The Stephanoses are still after her. Where is your place?" Trevor was already walking to the door when it burst open and Carmine

Stephanos stood in the doorway. "Never mind." He ended the call.

"Detective Stringer." Mr. St. Claire walked into the apartment behind his partner. "Where the hell is my daughter?"

Trevor casually put his phone in his back pocket, releasing the safety on his pistol resting in the holster at his side.

"She's safe." Trevor watched the two men advance on him, then walk right past. Carmine threw himself onto the couch, managing to look both bored and annoyed at the same time, while the councilman did a quick search of her bedroom and spare room.

"Why aren't you with her?"

"Why would her own father send hitmen after her?" Trevor countered the councilman. He'd been up against politicians his whole career, and he wasn't backing down this time. Too much rode on the outcome.

"Hitmen?" Stephanos laughed. He ran a fat hand over his overgrown belly and looked to St. Claire. "You really need to be better with your communication skills."

St. Claire ignored his cohort. "No one was trying to kill her. My daughter took some things that didn't belong to her. They were just trying to get them back."

"Really?" Trevor widened his stance, not expecting too much from these two, but being ready for anything. "So, the guys who barreled through the club, shooting at us weren't trying to kill her? The guy who showed up at her apartment, gun drawn, wasn't trying to kill her? Or how about when they blew up the cabin?" He couldn't help but yell the last question.

Carmine leaned forward, resting his elbows on his knees and settling a serious glare on Trevor. "The men I sent for her at the club have been dealt with, that much force was never authorized. My nephew followed you to her apartment, a shit hole from what he said, and he's still getting headaches from her bashing his head in. The fucking cabin was collateral damage. My men knew she wasn't inside. They checked first."

Trevor had seen plenty of men like Stephanos in his career. Calm demeanor but boiling rage simmered just below the surface. Anger at anyone who should dare step in his way. He also had an army of men ready to do his bidding. Not a great combination.

"What do you want with her anyway? What do you get out of this little marriage between your son and her?"

"Marriage?" Stephanos burst out laughing. "I wouldn't take that bitch into my family now for any amount of money. She's a snitch."

"Detective. I understand you spent some time with Addison, but you don't understand. She's been grieving over her fiancé and the marriage—"

"She knows Steven's alive." Trevor cut him off. It shouldn't feel that good to watch color drain out of a man's face.

"You were supposed to bring her home, not go digging into things that aren't your business." Spittle flew out the corner of the older man's mouth as he spoke. "You have fucked everything up!"

"You knew where she was, why didn't you go get her yourself?" Trevor focused his attention on the councilman.

"She wouldn't have come," St. Claire stammered, shooting a worried gaze to Stephanos who started to look more interested as the conversation continued.

"For two months, you knew where she was. You could have driven up there at a moment's notice to get her. Instead you waited. Why?" Trevor took a step toward St. Claire, somewhat blocking Stephanos' view of him. "You knew, didn't you? You knew Stephanos was getting tired of waiting, he wanted Addison and the information she had, and he wasn't going to wait anymore. That's why you called in a favor at the precinct. You didn't give a shit that you broke her heart with that stunt with Steven. You didn't care that she wanted to leave the city to follow her own dreams. But, I guess, I should give you a tiny bit of credit. Because you cared just enough to send someone to get to her before the Stephanos family did. Because you knew if they got her first, she wouldn't be coming home at all!"

ADDISON PUSHED OPEN the door to her apartment to find Trevor pointing a gun at Carmine Stephanos, and her father being held at gunpoint by Stephanos. Her father was empty handed. Not that she ever expected her father to dirty his own hands to get what he wanted done. No, that wasn't him. He had other people for that sort of work.

"Addison." Trevor didn't look over his shoulder at her when he barked her name. "Go back into the hallway."

"No. She comes inside." Stephanos cocked his pistol and twisted to point at Trevor, a near deafening sound when the barrel of the gun is pointed at a loved one.

"Addison. Outside." Not a fiber of Trevor's body reacted. Complete focus and control on the situation.

"This is absurd." Her father tried to step to the side, to go around Trevor but Stephanos quickly adjusted his aim and fired a warning shot, nearly taking out her father's knee, and effectively ruining her armchair.

"You stay there. Addison, come inside, and shut the fucking door." Stephanos kept his pistol aimed at her father, and ignored Trevor. "We're just going to talk."

"Addison. Go back out in the hallway. I won't say it

again." Trevor's demanding voice should have gotten her to obey immediately, except Stephanos pointed his gun at Trevor again.

"If I go, he'll shoot you." She did her best to sound annoyed. Like the whole affair was nothing more than an inconvenience, and not the terrifying moment that it was.

She didn't wait for a response. She shut and locked the door, dropping her bag with the few items Trevor had bought her in Michigan on the floor near the kitchen door.

"I don't have the file you're looking for." She walked over to the armchair, ignoring the bullet hole in the cushion as she sat her shaking body down.

"I know that," Stephanos sneered, still not taking his eyes off of Trevor.

"I won't have anything to do with your son."

"We already talked about that. I don't want a snitch in my family. I have enough enemies already."

"Then what is it you want?" Addison tried not to look at Trevor, but she could feel him, which was almost worse. The tension in the room grew as all three men watched each other, no one wanting to make the first move.

"I need to be sure you won't be doing anything stupid." Stephanos lowered his gun and waited for Trevor to do the same before facing her.

"Like go to the police?" Addison forced a laugh and

folded her hands in her lap, a futile effort to keep her hands from trembling. "Trevor is the police, and my father got him involved, not me. It wouldn't work anyway. This is Chicago and my father seems to have more influence than I ever believed. Besides, without my folder I have nothing to show them. It's just my word against Daddy's—and Daddy has done a good job at making me look the spoiled brat. That's all it would be seen as, a little rebellion." She noticed Trevor's shoulders stiffening when she mentioned being spoiled.

"She didn't make copies, and the electronic copies will be destroyed," Trevor stated. "The information she obtained was done so illegally. None of it would stand up in court, anyway. Not with the network of lawyers you both have on your payroll. I couldn't get an arrest warrant with it, even if I wanted to."

"And the fact that Steven is alive, I'm sure helps as well." She shot a glare at her father with her comment. The only response he had was to give a nervous look at the gangster standing beside him. "Oh. That's what he had on you? The favor you needed to repay him? He set up Steven's *death* and then later when his son wanted in my pants, you were obligated to pay up?"

"Shut up, Addison." Her father's snarl wasn't anything she hadn't experienced before. "I did you a favor getting rid of him. He was a sniveling coward. He didn't even let me finish my offer before he had the cash in his hands."

She ignored the twist of pain in her chest and rolled her shoulders back as she stood back up. "You did do me a favor." She nodded and quickly looked over at Trevor. His eyes were focused on Stephanos, but she could tell he was acutely aware of everything going on in the room. "I'll give you that. And you did send Trevor here to keep your buddies from killing me. I do owe you for that one, Daddy."

"Why did you have to make such a mess?" her father accused. "Everything would have been fine if you'd only done what I asked."

"Asked?" She fisted her hands at her sides and stepped up to her father. Stephanos be damned. "You never asked. Not once in my entire life. It's always been 'Addison, go to this school, Addison, date this man, Addison, get this degree. Addison, work here.' Not once have you ever asked."

Her father's eyes narrowed as he fixed them on her. Standing in front of her, he didn't look so big and strong anymore. He looked older, more gray streaking his hair, more wrinkles covering his face. And he didn't appear so scary with his trembling jaw and his thin frame.

"It was obvious you needed guidance. After I found that, that place where you met Steven. Really, Addison. If that's the sort of thing you'd like, I would think you would have been fine with being Jesse's wife. He can abuse you as much as you'd like."

Addison didn't speak. Her body tensed and her stomach twirled, but her vocal cords completely locked. She blinked a few times, letting the moment pass until she could form words again.

"Addison." Trevor's voice, smooth and calm, snaked its way into her mind.

She turned her back to her father and faced Stephanos, who looked intrigued and entertained by the family drama playing out before him.

"What do you need from me? I have no interest in you or my father. Steven's not dead, and I don't care about how corrupt you two are together." A calm settled into her body.

"Get out of Illinois." Stephanos shrugged. "That would be good enough for me. Your father—"

"Leave Illinois? Fine." She nodded and stuck out her hand to him. He didn't look so terrifying up close.

"You'll leave her alone if she stays out of Chicago?" Trevor grabbed Addison's arm and pulled her to his side. He'd let her handle Stephanos on her own. He could have grabbed her at any time, but he'd let her stand up for herself, and stood by her side the whole while. Because he never would have let anything happen to her.

"The state. She has to stay out of the state. I have

business dealings throughout Illinois, and I don't want her around to annoy me."

"She won't get in the way, Stephanos. I'll see to it," St. Claire chirped in.

"You know, St. Claire. You're as dirty as they come, and that's saying something in this city. And I'm not winning any father of the year awards, but it takes a real shithole to give up his kid the way you were going to with this one." Stephanos raked his gaze over her. "This girl has more integrity and more power than you'll ever have."

"What about the cabin?" Trevor pushed. Blake really was going to kill him over it.

Stephanos laughed and tucked his gun back into his pants. "Don't push it. And if I see your name anywhere near any legal action against me, you better believe this girl here will be the first person I visit." He pointed a fat finger at Addison.

"Not to worry," Trevor nodded.

Addison wanted to ask him why he would let them get away, but she already knew the answer. Because it would keep her safe. And that's what he did.

"Good." Stephanos ran his hand over his nearly bald head and gave Addison a toothy grin. "Then we have no trouble. You'll leave the state within the month, and you." He turned to her father who just stood there, gaping at them all. For once things weren't going his way and he was completely powerless to change it. "Are going to just keep things going as they were. But I think we'll have to renegotiate our rates." Stephanos patted his shoulder and walked out of the room.

Addison stood stoic until she heard the door close.

"Addy—"

"No." She shook her head and whipped around, stalking for the front door. Yanking it open, she pointed to the hallway. "Get out. Just go. I won't be your pawn anymore. Out."

Addison didn't bother looking at him. She'd never had a real father. It was losing the hope of having one in the future that hurt.

"I would suggest you get going, St. Claire," Trevor said.

Her father shuffled to the door, pausing only a moment when he reached her before walking out. "Let me know where you go. I want to be sure you're safe," he said as he passed through the door.

"I am safe. Without you, I'll be even safer." She slammed the door and bolted the lock, before resting her head against the door. There were no tears, no sobs for the loss of her father. All of those had been spent on him long ago. Only relief filled her soul. The ordeal was over. No one was hunting her any longer, she was free.

Now to deal with the angry beast standing in her living room.

19

Addison's shoulders slumped and her body slowly relaxed, though she continued to lean against the front door. Purging evil wasn't for the weak, and his Addison was anything but weak. She couldn't have made him prouder than how she handled herself. Although obeying his command to go back out into the hall would have been his preference, he could respect her need to handle the situation.

He may have lowered his weapon while they talked, but his finger had never left the trigger. One move, one breath too close to her, and Stephanos or her father would have eaten a bullet. No matter the consequence to him, he would see her safe and out of the clutches of anyone who posed a threat.

Now that they were gone, she looked limp. As

though every ounce of her energy had gone into that one confrontation, and she hadn't even fully looked at him yet.

"Addison." He approached her slowly, not wanting to startle her.

Her body tensed at the sound of his voice. "Trevor." Barely a whisper, but he could hear the anguish in his name.

"Baby."

"No." She shook her head and shoved off the door. "I think you should go, too." She put her hand on the knob but didn't turn it.

"What?" He stopped walking toward her; only three more steps and he could reach out and touch her.

She looked at him with red eyes, tears brimming but not falling. Her hair was pulled back into a pony- tail at the base of her neck, allowing him a view of the red blotches on her neck and cheeks.

"I think you should just go. It's all over with. You heard them, they'll leave me alone." Still her hand hadn't turned the knob.

"Addison, I'm not going anywhere." It was more than a statement; it was a vow. He'd never walk away from her, no matter how much she pushed.

"You know what? Fuck you." She shoved away from the door and pushed past him, her shoulder butting into his as she passed. He reached out and grabbed her arm, spinning her to face him.

"Language," he stated, dropping her hand when she yanked backward. She stumbled a few steps but caught herself.

"Fuck the language and fuck you."

"What are you so pissed at me for?" Obviously having to deal with her father and the Stephanos family was enough to fry her nerves, but he wasn't going to be her punching bag.

The question seemed to confuse her, like she wasn't sure of herself anymore.

"You lied to me about going to the car, you stole my car, and you drove straight into the city where the men who have been trying to kill you were waiting, and you're pissed at me?" He felt the muscles in his body seize up, his face grew hot. The woman had more nerve than she deserved at the moment. "You stole my car, Addison!" He all but yelled the statement at her.

"And you used me as some fuck toy!" she screamed back at him. Her cheeks flushed red, her eyes went wild with anger.

He took a step back, trying to process what she said. "What the hell are you talking about?"

"You didn't tell me about Steven right away." She jabbed a finger at him.

"No, I didn't." An explanation was probably in order.

"Because I may have stopped fucking you if I'd known he was alive." The words seem to rip through her, as her voice cracked along with her accusation.

"What? No." Of all the reasons he'd actually had, that one had never entered his mind. "That is absolutely *not* the reason I didn't tell you."

She stared at him, still struggling to breathe evenly. Taking a step forward, she pointed her finger once more and poked his chest hard. "Bullshit."

He captured her hand in his and held her close. "Did it ever occur to you that maybe it was something else? That maybe I was protecting you?"

Again, she yanked free of him, but this time she didn't step back.

"Right. You just wanted your free pussy to hang around as long as possible. What's one more fuck, right? That's what you thought?"

His temper started rising, nearly matching her glare. He couldn't blame her entirely for her train of thought. It looked bad, he knew it, but had nothing to do with wanting to get one more screw in.

"No! I know it looks that way, but I swear that wasn't it. I couldn't let him hurt you again, not like that. I'm sorry I didn't tell you right away. I was trying to protect you."

Her glare didn't soften. She'd shut him off, she wasn't hearing anything he said. He had to make her understand. Letting her dream up some sort of happily ever after with Steven in her mind only to have it shattered when she found out about the money, and how easily Steven had walked away would have been too much for him too.

If that made him a selfish ass, he'd agree. But he'd wanted to delay to keep her safe and protected for as long as he could.

"Addison, stop it, and listen to me." His voice lowered and he took a step back himself, because touching her now would be bad. For both of them.

"I don't have to anymore. You are relieved of protecting me. I'm home and I'm safe."

"Safe? You are still a loose end. You do one thing wrong, step in the direction of any police station, and Stephanos will have your head. You aren't safe until you're out of the state. And even then, it's going to be awhile before Stephanos really believes you aren't looking to fuck over your father. Because turning your father in is as good as turning *him* in."

A tear spilled over her lid, running down her cheek, and she swiped it away. Pushing the heels of her hands into her eyes, she growled and stomped her foot. Had the situation been different, he would have found the frustrated actions adorable.

"I won't be your little toy. You used me, and I've been used enough in my life." At least she wasn't yelling anymore, but her tone dove nose first into despair. The woman really thought she was just a plaything to him.

"Addison. I never used you. I never thought of you as just a fuck toy. I shouldn't have kept the information from you. I'm sorry for that, but I swear I didn't keep it to myself just so I could fuck you one more time."

She threw her fists to her sides and gave him another hard glare. "Then why? Why did you hold it from me?"

"Because." He took a deep breath. "If I had told you right away you would have been sitting for two days working up some romantic notion in your head that was never going to play out. The man took money to go away. When Blake told me about that money transfer—fuck, Addison, it took everything in me not to march into his house and just throw my fist into his face."

She was standing close enough to touch, but he couldn't, not yet. Emotions were still too raw, too tender.

"You knew why he left."

"I had a damn good idea, and if you'd fantasized about reuniting with him and—I couldn't let him hurt you like that. No fucking way. It was better to keep you in the dark until the last minute. Because even that much hurt, from what I saw was enough to warrant me killing the bastard."

"You didn't, did you? Kill him?"

Trevor sensed the tension easing but remained cautious. "No, of course not."

"You should have told me." Her voice firmed again, and she looked ready to get back into fighting him. It wasn't what she wanted or needed, though.

"I was doing what I thought was best, but I should have told you." He dragged his fingers through his hair. It wasn't complicated. In fact, nothing was more transparent in his entire life. "If he hadn't done what he did, didn't have a girlfriend now, would you be standing here yelling at me about this?"

"Is that why you were afraid to tell me?" A gentle turn of her lips suggested she was starting to find entertainment in his anguish.

"I wasn't afraid," he pointed out. "I worried."

"Why the hell would you worry?" She was poking again, searching for words he should have said days ago.

"Because you've been through enough pain on his account, on your father's account. I didn't want to lose you, of course I didn't. But if Steven had been an actual choice for you and you chose him, and he made you happy, I wouldn't stop you. It would fucking kill me, but I wouldn't have stopped you." He tapped one finger against her forehead. "Did it occur to you at all that I might have had your best interest in mind? Haven't I shown you that since I've met you? Even it means I lose, just so long as you win."

Though his actions came off rough, her smile widened.

"If not to keep your little fuck toy, then why?"

Was she not listening?

"Maybe because I actually like you." He grabbed her shoulders, pulling her against him, and his mouth hovered just over hers. "No, because I'm falling in love with you, you stubborn, bratty, sexy as fuck woman." And before she could ruin the moment, he brought his mouth down on hers.

HE'D KISSED her plenty of times over their brief time together, but never in any of those moments had she embraced the power he held over her as she did with that kiss.

Her arms hurt from his fingers digging into her flesh, but all she could focus on was the heated kiss. Everything blossomed within her. All her fears vanished, because he wasn't leaving her. He hadn't used her.

Her tongue ran over the bottom of her lip, trying to capture every bit of his taste. His eyes searched hers, dark and round. He hadn't shaved; stubble covered his jaw.

"You're falling in love with me?" Her own feelings

being mirrored by him would be too perfect. And her life didn't come with perfect.

"Fell. Falling fast. Whatever you want to call it." He let her arms go, and cupped her face. "How could you think I was just using you?"

"I-I'm not really used to people not using me." She tried to shrug it off, but he deserved more. "I was afraid, because I was feeling things for you and when I found out Steven was alive, I thought, well, I guess I got scared."

"If Steven didn't have a girlfriend, would we be here having this discussion?"

"When we got there, and he opened the door, I kept waiting for something to happen. Some spark to ignite again, but nothing happened. I was pissed, yeah, but nothing else happened. It hurt, but not as much as thinking you didn't want me, that what I thought had been developing had just been friends fucking friends."

"Friends fucking friends?" His lips parted in a wide grin and he kissed her, a quick peck. "I told you, I don't do this half assed, and I don't fuck my friends."

"Sort of like don't shit where you eat?" She tried to pull away when his eyes widened at her verbiage, but he only tightened his hold on her.

"Language. Second and last warning."

She closed her eyes, giving her senses time to catch up with her heartbeat. His warm hands were on her, his breath washed over her face, and the body heat from being so close to him intoxicated her. "Yes, Sir," she whispered and opened her eyes.

"You stole my car, sweet-cheeks." He took a step toward her, pushing her back a step, and continued to do this until he walked them into her bedroom.

"Yeah. Sorry about that?" She went with cute, maybe cute would work.

She should have known better.

"You swore at me several times." He walked her to the bed, until her legs hit the mattress, and she plunked down on her ass.

"I was angry," she pointed out as he went to the bedroom door and closed it. As though there was some audience in her living room he wanted to block out.

"You went right into the center of the trouble we were trying to get you out of." He stood in front of the door, his arms folded over his chest and his jaw set. A gentle shiver ran through her at the sight of dominance before her.

"No, I went to Charity's place. And no one came looking there," she pointed out. It had been a lucky gamble to stay with Charity for a few days. Her father knew where Charity lived, and he could have stopped there at any moment to see for himself if she was back or not.

"And today you barreled through that door to find both your father and Stephanos here."

"And you!" She pointed her finger at him.

"Of course, me!" Exasperation was just as hot as his irritated look, she decided.

"I don't want a punishment." There. Just name the damn elephant in the room. "I want you to make me feel good again. Make me feel like I'm yours."

He closed the distance between them and leaned over, placing his hands on the mattress on either side of her body and bringing his nose near touching hers. "You are mine, sweet-cheeks. Make no fucking mistake about that. I'm going to punish you; there's no getting around that. But not tonight. Not with so much gap between us."

His lips pressed against hers, pushing her to lie flat on the bed. His hands made quick work of removing her shirt, only breaking the kiss long enough to get the shirt over her head.

She scrambled back onto the bed when he gave her the room to do so while he removed his own clothing. She stripped out of her leggings, catching his grin when she revealed she'd gone commando.

"What? You didn't buy me enough underwear."

"I only bought what you needed." He slid his hands under her arms and pushed her back up on the bed, shoving her legs open with his knee. Her skin trembled beneath his warm fingers as they made their way along her thighs, tracing her hips, and moved further up to her chest. "And you don't need panties."

Any protest she may have feigned disappeared when he kissed her and thrust into her. She moaned into his mouth, arching her back and taking him further.

"Sweet-cheeks, you're so fucking wet." He thrust again harder and harder as her body shifted and adjusted to his strength, craving more of it.

"Trevor, please." She pulled her legs back, spreading her thighs further and smiling as his eyes rolled and at the uncontrolled growl he let loose.

"No, not yet." He reached between their bodies, finding her clit and brushing his fingers so gently over it she shuddered. "You'll wait until I say, or you'll have another punishment coming." His orders were firm. They may be closing the gap between them, reconnecting, but that didn't diminish his power over her.

"Yes, Sir." She'd promise him anything and everything.

"You're so good," he breathed against her mouth, between kisses. He thrust hard again, making her cry out into his mouth. "So good." He pressed his forehead against hers.

"Trevor," she moaned as she arched her body, lifting her hips to meet his thrust and taking the hard length of him. "Please, Sir, oh—Trevor." Her insides shook with need. Her body craved his permission and would not give until she heard the words.

He captured her hands and pinned them over her head with one fist. "Take what I give, sweet-cheeks."

"Yes." She nodded, unable to see his face clearly because of his close proximity, but she could still make out the tension in his jaw. He was unraveling as quickly as she was.

He grunted as he pulled back and drove hard into her, filling her completely and stretching her instantaneously. She cried out from the force, but kept her legs parted, and watched his expression darken as he pulled back once more to thrust into her.

Her cry was lost between his own growl and the sound of their bodies meeting with their thrusts. While keeping her hands pinned over her head, he reached down between them and flicked her clit again and again.

"Come for me, baby. Come as much as you want." He hooked his arm under her knee, pulling her leg up toward her and driving further than ever before.

It was enough to send her over the edge. The bite of pain as he drove deep into her spread her release throughout her body, sending waves of pleasure to every inch of her. She screamed out into the room, her eyes flying open and connecting with his as he too pushed over the edge and took his orgasm head on.

He let go of her wrists and kissed her again, this

time on the cheek then her jaw until he made his way to her mouth. His chest pressed against hers, letting her feel his heat and his hard body.

"So beautiful," he whispered, slipping from her body and settling beside her. He leaned up on his elbow and wiped a strand of hair from her face. "Even more after you've had a good fucking." He smiled, and the little dimple on his cheek appeared. How had she ever thought this man looked so menacing?

"Don't get all mushy on me now." She nudged his shoulder.

"Never." He feigned a serious expression. "But I plan on spoiling you even more rotten than I accused you of being, and bringing you down a few pegs when you get too big of a head."

She sighed. "Sounds wonderful."

"It will be, sweet-cheeks."

20

A ttendance on a Friday night at Leather and Lace usually didn't ramp up until around ten, and it was only nine. Addison felt pretty confident Trevor and she would have the main room mostly to themselves. An audience didn't sound appealing in the least. There was enough concern with going through what Trevor had promised her, let alone worrying about peering eyes.

"You're nervous." Charity grinned while helping to pin up Addison's hair. Another command of Trevor's; he didn't want any hair getting in his way.

"Of course I am," Addison bit back.

"He's not going to hurt you—well, I mean he is, but—"

Addison patted her longtime friend's hand as it

rested on her shoulder. "I know, Charity. I'm not nervous about that. This whole thing is nerve-racking. Moving to Michigan, starting a new job, being with Trevor full time. It's a lot of change real fast."

"Yeah." Charity nodded then went about finishing the up-do. "But staying here isn't going to work. Besides, you said his brother owns a BDSM resort up there. Apparently, Jackson served with him back in his military days. He'll make sure we get up there plenty of times."

Leave it to Charity to find the silver lining.

"I know. It's just a lot."

"Do you think that's why he waited this long?"

"For tonight?" Addison stepped away from the mirror in the locker room and faced Charity. "He wants our new beginning to have a clean slate. Besides, I guess it took this long for him to stop being so damn pissed about that car."

"You stole his car, Addy. Jackson said you're lucky all you're getting is this."

"You listen to Jackson too much."

Charity laughed. "I have more fun when I do than when I don't. A lesson you'd do well to learn sooner rather than later." Charity brushed her own wavy hair over her shoulders. "You better not keep him waiting too long."

"You aren't going to watch, are you?"

The blush told her everything. "I wasn't given a choice."

"This just got worse."

"I think that might be the point." Charity linked her arm through Addison's and started walking toward the door. "It will be fine."

Addison didn't have as much confidence when she opened the door and found the lounge already half full of people. Searching the crowd, she came up empty. Where was he?

"Did he call everyone he knew?" she groaned.

"This is between you and him. I don't think this crowd has anything to do with you. It might have everything to do with free membership night though." Charity pointed to the flier pinned to the wall. Every now and then Leather and Lace did a free guest pass night for members.

Trevor may not have called for an audience, but he'd picked the perfect night for one.

Charity left Addison's side once they walked through the lounge and entered the main room. Trevor was already in position, standing beside the St. Andrews cross. Wearing only his jeans, he held his belt in his hand, snapping it against his thigh. She caught his gaze as she began to move toward him, no longer aware of the crowd behind her in the lounge.

The spotlight over the cross would provide Trevor

with enough light to see the marks he laid across her body, as well as anyone stopping to watch her punishment play out.

When she reached him, he gave her a nod and pointed to the robe she wore. Without hesitation, she slid it from her shoulders and draped it across the table set up beside the play station.

"I'm not going to bind you. You are going to hold on to the cuffs I have hanging for you, and you are going to accept your punishment. If you move out of position, more will be added."

"Yes, Sir." She nodded. He expected her to offer herself for her discipline, to accept his authority in punishing her, and she would give it freely.

The wood platform beneath the cross was cool beneath her bare feet as she stepped into position. Reaching up for the leather cuffs dangling from the upper rings of the cross, her naked breasts pushed against the cushion nestled in the center. Her nipples hardened at the crisp feel of the leather. Cool as she was at the moment, she'd be simmering once he started.

"Tell me why we are here." He stepped to her side, gripping her at the back of her neck. He didn't push on her neck to make her look up at him, but instead held her steady so as to keep her eyes straight ahead.

"I ran away from you. I stole your car, and drove right into danger with it."

"Will you do it again?" The question came with sincerity and great concern. The lesson needed to be learned that consequences followed bad actions.

"No, Sir. I will never steal your car again." She tried to keep the hint of humor from her voice, but the tightness of his grip signaled to her she'd failed.

"Well, we'll see how cheery you are after you're done with your punishment. What is your safeword?"

"Master," she whispered, knowing even without using it she'd be safe.

"That's right, sweet-cheeks." He patted her naked bottom with his hand. "No counting, just take it and learn from it. Got it?"

"Yes, Sir."

"Good." He released her neck and moved his position again. She settled herself, gripping the cuffs harder.

At first, he peppered her backside with his hand. Flat, hard slaps that covered her entire ass. He didn't speak, or lecture; he'd done enough of that already. This moment was only for accepting her consequence. For them to clear the air and rid it of the scent of disobedience between them.

Just as her ass began to warm and she started to fall into a pleasant haze, a sharp crack of the belt landed, jostling her from the comfortable place in which she'd settled. Another fell, and another. One after the other he laid the belt across her ass, covering her every inch from top to bottom.

She began to wiggle, to find some small reprieve from the burn of the leather, but his hand pressed against her back, holding her against the cushion and keeping her where he wanted her. The strikes came harder, with less time between them.

She cried out, pulling down on the cuffs. "Oh!" She stomped her foot, but he wasn't deterred. He moved down toward her thighs, sending new lines of electric fire through her body.

"I'm sorry! So sorry!" she yelled, but if he heard her it changed nothing.

His body pressed against her hip, his arm now wrapped around her waist and held her completely immobile against him. She could feel the tension, the slick layer of sweat building on his chest as he continued to punish her.

A jangle of the belt, then more lashes. Less sting and more thud—he'd doubled the belt again. But the smaller implement gave him more control over where he struck. Not an inch of her backside and thighs was left untouched and the tears flowed easily.

Hard sobs were racking her body, and she wiggled and turned, but he held her.

"Almost, baby, almost there," he said into her ear. "Doing so good for me, baby."

"Please," she begged but his only response was to give a harder lash.

Just when she thought the fire burnt too hot, when she couldn't take another lick, he threw the belt to the floor.

She rolled her head to the side, resting it on his shoulder as he continued to hold her. She cried. Not quiet little tears of self-pity, but hard sobs of regret and remorse.

His hand ran over her raw, aching flesh, and he kissed her head, letting her cry as much as she needed.

"Come here, love." He turned her, picking her up as she wrapped her arms around his neck. He carried her to the chairs behind the station; a few people had to move to give him space. Where had everyone come from? She hadn't heard any of them.

Trevor sat down, cradling her in his arms. The brush of his jeans against her swollen ass made her suck in her breath, but it was nothing compared to the release of everything that had been built up because of her actions.

He held her. He didn't prod her for words, or push her to hurry up, he just held her, resting his chin on her head.

When she finally calmed, the tears stopped and she could breathe evenly, she pushed away and looked at him. "I'm so sorry. I almost—I almost messed it all up."

He kissed the tip of her nose, not even being bothered by the tears and sweat that covered her face. "I'm sorry, too. We need to take care of each other, Addison. And that means always being honest, no matter how scared we are about what the result will be."

"Yes, Sir." She nodded, swiping the back of her hand across her cheek.

"And you didn't almost mess anything up. No way I was letting you go, not so easily." He hugged her tighter. "You're perfect for me, Addison. I couldn't imagine this any other way, with anyone else."

"You're giving up your job," she pointed out.

"In this town, corruption runs rampant, and I'm only one man. It's a smaller unit, but I think being a detective in Michigan is going to be much more rewarding. Besides, Devin is going to love having us around."

She looked him in the eyes, searching for some flaw she'd missed. Nothing but love. No agenda behind his words, no ultimatum if she didn't play by his rules—well, except the discipline. But even that was all her choice, under her power, and it was given with such love even the burning pain of the belt couldn't keep her away from him.

"I fucking love you, Trevor." The emotion shook her, it was so forceful.

He grinned. "Language."

She yelped at the pinch he gave her ass, and snuggled back into his neck.

"I love you, too, sweet-cheeks."

Thank you for reading Protecting His Runaway. I hope you loved meeting Trevor and Addison. The Owned and Protected Series continues with His Captive Pet.

THANK YOU

Stormy Night Publications would like to thank you for your interest in our books.

If you liked this book (or even if you didn't), we would really appreciate you leaving a review on the site where you purchased it. Reviews provide useful feedback for us and our authors, and this feedback (both positive comments and constructive criticism) allows us to work even harder to make sure we provide the content our customers want to read.

If you would like to check out more books from Stormy Night Publications, if you want to learn more about our company, or if you would like to join our mailing list, please visit our website at:

http://www.stormynightpublications.com

ADDITIONAL BOOKS IN THE OWNED AND PROTECTED SERIES

Protecting His Pet

After her brother's life of crime is brought to a sudden end, twenty-two-year-old Kara Jennings fears she may be the next target of the men who killed him. It comes as a shock, however, when she is taken captive by a mysterious man who promises to keep her safe but quickly demonstrates that he will not hesitate to punish her in any way he sees fit if she disobeys him.

Devin Stringer is certain there is something important that Kara is refusing to share with him—something related to her brother's death—and he is fully prepared to be as firm as necessary to get her to tell him the truth, even if that means stripping her bare, spanking her soundly, and keeping her caged like a pet.

Despite her shame at being made to kneel naked at her captor's feet, eat from his hand, and surrender her body to him completely, Devin's dominance leaves Kara helplessly aroused and yearning for him to master her even more thoroughly. When he brings her to the edge of an intense climax only to leave her desperate and wanting, her need for him to claim her properly compels Kara to confess the secret her brother shared with her before his death. But will that information help Devin protect his beautiful pet or will it ultimately put her in greater danger?

ABOUT THE AUTHOR

Measha Stone is a USA Today Bestselling romance author who loves reading almost as much as writing. You can often find her either at her computer or curled up with a book and a hot cup of coffee. Her books range from loving BDSM to a darker side of the genre, but no matter where in the spectrum of erotic romance you find her, there will always be an Alpha Male Dominant right there with her- and that happily ever after we all crave. She likes to write submissive women who are strong willed, and fully capable of taking life by the horns. Not much is sweeter than a strong woman bending to the will of her mate, except for maybe the Dominant who bends her!

Measha lives in the suburbs of Chicago with her husband and three children. Although she works hard on her writing, and reads every chance she gets, spending time with her family is a high priority. Even if that entails binge watching old sitcoms on Netflix with the kids curled up around her and her husband dishing out the popcorn.